AF269045

Feral Architecture:
Ballardian Horrors
Edited by Sam Richard

Contents

Foreword
Scott Dwyer

"Fiction is a branch of neurology: the scenarios of nerve and blood vessels are the written mythologies of memory and desire."

In the 1970's science fiction writer J.G. Ballard started crafting what may be the most disturbing and interesting work in science fiction ever to have been written. In what has been termed his "concrete trilogy": *Crash*, *High-Rise*, and *Concrete Island*, along with his experimental novel *The Atrocity Exhibition*, Ballard pushed the boundaries of what science fiction could be, and took a deep dive into a society on the verge of collapse and the inherit self-destructive desires of the people who live in that society. Personal, abstract, perverse, obsessive, brilliant. Work this shockingly honest and so deeply disturbed and perverted had never been written in science fiction before. With Ballard's Concrete Trilogy, a modern mythos of erotic tales of ruin and breakdown, both personal and technological, was born.

To give a brief description of these essential books: *Crash* explores all the erotic possibilities of the human body damaged and deformed by modern technological disasters like the car crash. *The Atrocity Exhibition* is an abstract examination of a person lost in a dehumanized landscape of pornography and media. *High-Rise* is a venture into the darkness of suburban life and a return to a savagery looming, hidden, in customer service and modern-day comforts. *Concrete Island* is a modern-day Robinson Crusoe, except stranded in the unseen areas hidden in our modern cities.

There is a blend of horror and sci-fi in his works that mirror Ballard's love of surrealism. The juxtaposition of two different objects. A sewing machine and an umbrella. Car crashes and pornography. Putting the dark side of our subconscious dreams and traumas under his microscope, Ballard's work let's our deepest nightmares, or maybe fantasies, out to play.

Ballard, despite being normally seen as a science fiction author, has had an enormous influence on horror fiction and cinema. David Cronenberg took subtle influence for *Videodrome* and took direct influence for his adaptation of *Crash*. Michael Blumlein's fiction, especially his collection *The Brains of Rats*. The alienated media obsessive in Dan Gilroy's film *Nightcrawler*. The desire for self-destruction in von Trier's film *Antichrist*. The vertiginous science fiction tales of Brian Evenson. Traces of Ballard's influence can be felt in all these works as well as many others.

Ballard is the 20th century poet of ruin and breakdown. But also, Ballard is by heart in his writing an optimist. He sees the possibilities of pleasure and transcendence in the car crash and the pornographic film. He views the dehumanization of humanity with a gleeful eye. His work is shocking, and a lot of the power of his work is his embracing of this post-human future we seem to be racing towards.

In our current state of media environments and alienating worlds of social media, we find ourselves living in a media produced fiction. And now more than ever we need stories, we need fantasy, to help us find real truth. We need fiction to help us find ourselves, all the mirrors seem to be broken and self-reflection has been taken over by Disney and Superhero narratives. The horror genre is one of the few avenues we have left for honest artistic expression and exploration. Ballard championing of surrealism, pornography, perversion, and the embracing of the darkest parts of ourselves as a means to liberate and find ourselves, can serve as a kind of mission statement for modern day horror literature.

> "Sex is now a conceptual act, it's probably only in terms of the perversions that we can make contact with each other at all."

Paranoid Cancers of a Demented Eros

Joe Koch

The Bride Stripped Backward

Teagan planned to resign from the project even before the spinning black razorblades altered and replaced the reflecting pool's still surface in the peace garden, so named as an inside joke. Strife spilled out of the multi-storied office building and its cultish laboratories into that formerly landscaped corporate meditation space. He and Martine christened it ironically, sharing droll glances behind Dr. Oswald's back, or so he thought. The invasiveness of Oswald's perception, strengthened in lucid dream states and evidenced by the myriad blades now clicking fitfully in ascending spirals, had escaped detection until it was too late to confront him without fatal violence.

Teagan refused to feel regret. He threw the last

bite of his protein bar at the tide of motile black planes, vexed that he'd lost track of Martine's whereabouts again. Where did she vanish to? Had she found Oswald, or his body? The sculpted pool that once mirrored the surrounding sky and towers surged blackly at the bite of food. The dead mobility of its surface action offered no reflection.

Steely black edges deleted the protein bar's mass, not so much slicing it as vanishing portions into a slick void. Intrigued, Teagan leaned nearer, tempted to penetrate the vacuum with an exploratory finger. Birdsong and insects from the complex's overgrown lawns suggested no danger to the organic molecular structure of flesh, but only to things inert.

He hesitated. Not because their work was inconclusive, but because Teagan didn't trust Dr. Oswald, either alive or dead. He must caution Martine more strongly against her solitary forays if he failed to convince her to leave.

Could he go through with it, though? He had to. The project had veered out of control. Isolation from Dr. Oswald, both imperative and impossible, hadn't been accomplished by geographical distance or disabling sedation. If Oswald had survived the medically induced coma—and mustn't he have, since his body had disappeared?—Teagan had little faith he or Martine could argue against him in a way that would matter. His mind was too far out of reach.

Should never have tried to kill him, Teagan thought, *or done a better job.*

Yet even now, the idea of outright aggression, of bludgeoning or cutting the man felt like a blow to his own gut. Maybe his resolve to quit was mere pathetic self-deception. The seeker in him wanted to stay on and follow Oswald's oblique line of thought further, deeper, all the way to the unreasonable end. As the sound of black razorblades reconstructed a sense of cold dread in Teagan's chest, he sought his reflection in the flickering voids of the transformed pond and trembled with equal fear and hope that Oswald wasn't really dead.

Corruption of the Fittest

She ran over the thing with the jeep on her way to check the station at the reservoir. Throwing on heavy leather work gloves—she hadn't thought to travel with a biohazard suit—Martine grabbed a crowbar in case it was still moving. Although something weighty and iron in her hands made her feel more powerful, her negotiation skills, commitment, and intelligence were the true attributes keeping her safe. Oswald had trusted her, continued to trust her, even now after the breach—but she couldn't depend on his good grace, not indefinitely. Sooner or later, Oswald, or whatever echo of his mind persisted with her into the physical present, was bound to turn on her. Perhaps the thing in the road was evidence he already had.

The tumor was a clay-like pink, the color of brick. More translucent than the lab-grown specimens, it behaved in a way she found surprisingly tame. She crouched down and observed its senile directionless movements and how its epithelial layer leaked, picking up dirt that turned into a film of mud.

She nudged it—not too hard—with the crowbar. Reflexively tensed for an attack, she very nearly crushed it to pulp on the rocky embankment when it jolted forward and seized onto the crowbar. She took a deep breath. It clung there, quivering.

Gelatinous pseudopods encircled the titanium tip. The tumor kneaded as if suckling. It reminded Martine uncomfortably of a newborn puppy or kitten.

Mutation in the wild was an entirely new development, and that excited her. It might be the awakening they had worked for. More importantly, an independently evolving specimen suggested a shift in the collapse, heralding a new route into understanding Oswald's unconscious desires and manipulating the material consequences of his projections.

The project could be saved. Proof nursed on the

end of the crowbar.

Martine was ready to take the next step.

In Obsidian Monarchies, Our Infection doth Glitter

Dr. Oswald's dream cantilevered the towering central skyscraper into a horizontal mesh that gored the buildings around it. Starting from the top, girders fanned outward in multiple opposing directions like an exploded steel skeleton. Glass panes slid and refracted like crystalline growths over the inverse ends of tiers below. Vast sections of reinforced concrete folded. Platforms jutted across diagonal gradations, piling downward in illogical defiance of geometry and physics, upending load-bearing supports. The diseased tower spread and grew with the lively imbalance of a colony of cancer cells bathed in radiation.

Havoc erupted from the intersections of impossible angles as the building re-patterned. The human cost was minimal. Most of the staff had left headquarters weeks ago when Dr. Oswald disappeared and the architecture started behaving unpredictably.

Everyone here knows the risks, Teagan reassured himself, crouching beside the reflecting pond where he'd found no reflection. It was what Oswald would say, wasn't it? And anyone left who had witnessed the colossal mutations understood the hazardous effects without needing to know their true cause.

Oswald's uncontrolled cataleptic projections continued restructuring the skyscraper with the force of an earthquake. The reflecting pond rose into a black shimmering tower as the office building shifted into horizontal instability, unsettling the surrounding towers. Spared by his dalliance, Teagan was saved from crashing debris and thrusting girders by the deleting action of the black edges of the pool's spinning blades.

Martine might be anywhere, he realized, huddling beneath the black clicking spiral. What if she'd heeded his advice and given up her mysterious journeys, returning at this very moment?

Then Teagan panicked. What if she'd found Oswald? What if they were both inside, Martine helpless in his arms as he wreaked his madman's vengeance?

Melismos: Strange Messages in the Garbage

"We must teach the environment to fight back," Oswald said, raising a firm yet temperate fist for emphasis. His lectures were notorious. "Conservation mandates, ecoterrorism, nothing's gone far enough, has it? Trying to restore a lost balance is as useless and abstract as trying to turn back a clock; sheer fantasy. No, nature must learn anew to fight for survival." His voice lowered. His tall frame bowed, gently targeting the most receptive of his students. "We can be teachers. Turn illness into a weapon."

Oswald's colleagues joked that he was building a cult. By the end of the second year, he was. Assembling a loyal research team that not only applied his concepts to chemistry, mechanical engineering, genetics, and biology, but that also had the acumen to secure a generous corporate sponsorship, he left university without tenure and went private.

Martine was instrumental in recruiting and gaining sponsors. Although she maintained that purulent speculation was irrelevant, she'd been Dr. Oswald's star student, then his assistant, and then his rumored romantic partner, and intrigue about the relationship fueled a certain titillating notoriety Martine didn't hesitate to exploit. Furthermore, without her knack for translating Oswald's abstruse goals into laymen's terms, he would never have been able bring the necessary language of financial credence to his disputed ideas.

Leading an exodus of graduates and post-doc fellows, they settled on an abandoned suburban office park far from town. Manicured lawns sprawled between gleaming skyscrapers. Empty, arid plains disappeared into the distance beyond gated borders.

Only the reservoir and a smattering of isolated mobile homes in the foothills could be glimpsed from the topmost floors. To further limit contagion, all but the central tower remained unoccupied, serving as buffers for the headquarters and its labs.

In this, the tallest of the buildings, Oswald took up residence in the top story office suite, even though he despised the bland excess of the modern complex. He insisted on a contractual clause forbidding maintenance of the grounds, allowing the lawns to re-wild. Once the lessors transferred temporary liability, he disabled the outdoor sprinkler system. As Oswald refused now, as he always had, to waste fuel by commuting, he rarely had reason to leave the tower. His followers soon took to calling it The Castle.

Teagan flinched. The metaphor ate at his nerves. Of course Oswald was king. He had no argument with that. But with Martine as the obvious queen, Teagan was left out in the middle of nowhere. He was stuck between two figureheads, lovers who were also his lovers in the strange dynasty they'd established. At best his place was comic, the role of the jack, or court jester.

The Clown King in Yellow

The first architectural cancers that escaped the lab must have hitchhiked on jewelry, zippers, or pocket change; perhaps the odd shoe eyelet or bobby pin. Modeled on the human papilloma virus, the infections carried various synthetic and metallic polymer replicating disruptor codes harmless to organic life such as humans and animals, but—as Oswald's ideas actualized shockingly into material fact over the course of the project—destructive to the vast majority of manufactured products polluting the environment, piling up in landfills, and choking the oceans.

Eradicating pollution was the public project goal. Insiders knew Oswald had more radical plans. By infecting host animals, insects, and plants in protected areas, these important targeted tracts of land could resist real estate development, fracking, pipelines, and so on. Wildlife habitat would become physically inviolable. Sacred ground would no longer be stolen and exploited. The earth, as Oswald said, would learn to fight back.

"Perhaps we were too careless," Martine admitted in a harsh tone once the breach came to light. She didn't take criticism well, especially not from him. He wasn't himself, seemed to be in some kind of aggressive, manic state.

"Oh, do you think so?" Teagan's voice, typically intimate and gentle, now bristled with sarcasm. "Thorannsson nearly died. His car, the pay phone, I don't know; maybe he touched a credit card machine at the gas station while he was waiting. How the hell do you contain that?"

Martine sat behind her desk, an elbow on each armrest, hands folded, eyes on fire hiding her shock. She held very still to stop her heart racing and slow her breath. Something about him felt terribly off, terribly wrong. She smiled without humor. "Are we done here?"

"Darling, don't shut me out. Not now. Not like this."

No One Cries for the Canticle Horse: a Fenestration

Before nearly colliding with the semi, Thorannsson's focus was split three ways between a rattle from his second-hand Toyota's engine, excitement about his viral sequencing script, and dread he couldn't put off telling Calvin he'd agreed to work on their son's birthday.

It wasn't that work was more important than family. Of course not. But Thorannsson was on the brink of a breakthrough. He couldn't leave anything to chance. Surely Calvin could agree a three-year-old hardly knows the difference.

A new clank punctuated the engine rattle, interrupting his train of thought. At the same time,

Thorannsson's phone began—well, not ringing; he didn't know how to explain it later. He felt a distinct sensation of something out of place. The compartment of the car *tightened*. In the breast pocket of his jacket, the phone rumbled like stones grinding together. The fabric ripped. Something angular jabbed at his chest. At the same time, an insistent pressure garbled in his ears, demanding attention. No known ringtone or emergency alert, no *sound*, but the idea of noise battered against space and strained to take shape.

Thorannsson fought to extract the phone from his pocket. He steered with his knee. The case jutted and somehow *doubled* through layers of cloth. He ripped it out, though it shifted unnaturally in his palm. Holding the phone high, he tapped at the shattered screen.

Nothing.

He squinted.

Something in the cracks.

The screen dissected into protruding and refracting layers. Thorannsson swiped. Nothingness blinked back at him. The device hummed. In the blackness between broken edges, in a kaleidoscope of tiny fault lines, messages unmade meaning. Euhedral faces flashed and vanished that he couldn't make sense of, letters and symbols denied or forgotten, hieroglyphs that prematurely aged his eyes out of focus. The sensation of noise prickled on his scalp.

Horns blared. He looked up. The road was fractal.

Thorannsson swerved onto what he thought was a curb and went straight into oncoming traffic.

Crystallizing lenses corroded his view. His eyeglass frames bored into his temples like miniature vice grips. He yanked them off.

Something stung his eye. A rush of tears blinded him. Later he'd learn he was lucky the multidirectional expansion of polymer and metal growths hadn't gouged out his eyes.

He swung the wheel to the left. The car plowed into a gulch and stalled.

As the semi-truck blew past, Thorannsson knew he should be horrified and not elated. He'd had a close brush with death. But the phone and eyeglasses that metastasized visibly into unstable configurations of their synthetic components like devices adapting to some alien dimension's specifications proved his success. His viral sequence had worked.

Oswald was going to be so proud.

The Single Sparkling Eye of the First Fish in Flight

Martine lifted the tire iron. The tumor clung as if suckling.

She pulled, but her heavy leather gloves made it

difficult to maneuver. Although the composition of its "body"—really an amorphous, semi-translucent, multi-lobed lump with no central nervous system—gave in to pressure as if it were pliable and weak, the urgent clasp of its pseudopods held tight to the crowbar.

Nothing about this life form—and she had to call it life, because it behaved like life, like a thing with drives, desires, and needs—made sense to Martine. Since Oswald's outburst, it had become impossible to distinguish between mutations caused by escaped viral syntheticarcinoma materials and the manifestations of repressed unconscious errata projecting into physical reality from the depths of Oswald's dreams.

She reconsidered the import of her lover's puzzling, morose ramblings after their last ill-fated threesome, mere days before Thorannsson's crash revealed the breach.

"It's not that I don't find you beautiful," he said, his eyes clouded, his cock softened. It curled back into him like a shy animal. "Quite the opposite. You represent everything I love about women's bodies, not only in appearance and form, but in the way you move. The way you react to things, hold yourself. Or let go. I love to watch you and hear you—smell you—when he evokes your response.

"He shapes you as I guess he has shaped all of us. But you most, at those moments of mutual orgasm when the two of you sort of *break*; and I'm terrified, I'm sorry, I don't know what to say. I can't bear to touch you anymore."

Teagan looked up at Martine in earnest, unable to read her face. Her beautiful, perfect face. She was everything he'd ever wanted. "It's not me. It's not even you," he said. "It's him."

Did she nod? He continued regardless, propelled by the momentum of his confession.

"I want him. I have never wanted a man. I'm not like that. You brought me here. And I'm so grateful for that, darling. But I want him. I want his old, unstable body with its asymmetries and paunch and scars, his wrinkled cock, his nearsightedness, his cough. I want this landscape of memories embedded in him. I want to drink from his mind as from a cup.

"I'm destroyed when he's inside me. I become the ground, the dirt, and it's so far beyond beauty. I'm real with him like I never have been. And when it's over, I wonder: am I still real? Was I ever?

"Am I one of Oswald's untested theories that his genius dreamed up? But if I touch you and you're real —and look, you are; I know what's next. It means we're growing a new earth. It needs new creatures capable of destroying it."

He was hard by the time he finished. Martine ceased pacing naked around the divan, still frowning.

She stood over him, looked him up and down. Then she smiled and slapped his face. Hard. He moaned.

Martine's teeth gleamed.

She threw her head back in a boisterous laugh. Next she leaned close and said, "Don't you dare touch me. Not one finger. Turn your head so I can't feel you so much as breathe."

Now, holding the tumor, remembering how hard she'd milked him though they were already raw, how he'd disconcertingly screamed his own name instead of hers, how it hurt in a necessary way she didn't fully understand, and how after it was over the semen that overflowed from her rectum crystallized on the divan's plush into a series of radiant ivory cubes slipping into geometrical absurdity, proliferating without direction, and erupting in fleeting steeples; how they warped into grasping forms mimicking marbled flesh; and then how all their shared discharge crumbled into a microscopic model of a sick globe poisoned by the endgame of an ideological plastic mental crisis; considering all this, Martine threw off the heavy leather gloves she wore to forestall contamination—why not race toward the inevitable?—and seized the clinging, infantile thing off the tire iron's moistened tip.

Damp as a sponge in her hand, the softball-sized tumor clutched at the air with pseudopods formed on a central paramecium-like oblong, amorphously seeking new paths with each pleading gesture. It was the opposite of the architectural cancers envisioned by Oswald, an answer to what had escaped from the lab.

Oswald might dream a robust ecology overtaking technology weakened by disease, but he had not dreamed this.

She unbuttoned her cargo shirt down to the navel and lifted out her left breast. A small pockmark opened in the center of the spongy tumor between the squirming, rudimentary appendages. The hole depressed, grew wider, and puckered open and closed with soft wet sounds that made Martine's skin flush. Warmth flooded her pelvic floor. She cupped the tumor and held it to her chest. Eagerly, it latched.

Through the Negation of Negation, the Impossible Is Imagined as a Nearly Human Act

Teagan entered Dr. Oswald's coma. Deconstructing actualizations bloomed with inverse geometry. He rushed inside to rescue Martine as the building's outlandish mutations teetered on the cusp of instability.

No door existed. The Castle unfolded horizontally more so than vertically, its massive beams dividing at specious angles to form a series of interpenetrating deformed cubes. Teagan climbed the exterior, noting many cavities, wondering if the permeability of the reformulated tower signified Oswald's death or his comatose brain's decline.

Surely he hadn't survived.

Oswald's barbiturate habit had made it easy to experiment with higher doses to suppress the dangerous projections with deeper, longer sleep. When that failed, Teagan induced coma, augmenting Oswald's pheno with propofol. Of course he didn't tell Martine. Each time Teagan upped the dosage or frequency of sedation, the irrational architecture and technological grotesqueries abated, but only temporarily.

In a way, Teagan had admired him more than ever when he administered that final dose. Even in coma, Oswald's subconscious had unstructured reality, rushing the syntheticarcinogenic viral effects forward toward total technological collapse. From every confrontation, the force of Oswald's mind had emerged triumphant. As Teagan pushed the fatal dosage in, hands shaking so much he fumbled twice at placing the needle, he truly didn't know if he was more hopeful or fearful that Oswald might be too powerful to die.

It had never occurred to him Oswald might keep dreaming after death.

The Phenomenological Threshold of Meat

If neither coma nor death could stop Oswald, and if Teagan could not tell the difference between physical infection and diseased dream, how could he hope to contain the cancers they'd made?

Perhaps it doesn't matter in the face of extinction, he thought, just as Teagan's individual desires didn't matter when measured against the enormity of Oswald's vision. All desire was the property of Dr. Oswald, a complex of unanimous will, stolen and redirected, powering the earth, poised to save the environment through hyper-immunity. Even now, trying to distinguish internal from external, joining with Oswald's creation, becoming part of the interstitial spaces that presented egress as he crawled over malformed glass tetrahedrons and slipped through confounding spirals of rebar and crashed concrete, he felt his ambition give way to the genius of a greater loss.

"Martine," he said, though the name gave him no anchor.

He felt a sudden pang of freedom in the delusional, catastrophic space, as if the threesome's emotional trap was made manifest by the building's obscene complexity. A sharp whiff of familiar pleasure: the gratification of playing a role with no known parameters. In the complete disruption of reality, the trap turned inside-out and exposed its workings in a liminal divide, leaving Teagan no stage, no script, and no rules. Strangely, he felt grounded and clear.

It was never Martine. He enjoyed her degradations; even relished being shared and traded between the two, but it wasn't for her that he returned to The Castle. It was for Oswald. It had always been Oswald.

"Oswald," a voice rasped, as if echoing Teagan's thoughts.

He started, nearly lost his bearings. Through the crazed jungle-gym of deconstructed architecture, he spotted Thorannsson.

Teagan gaped at the complete overthrow of symmetrical logic in the planes of Thorannsson's body. He hardly recognized him as human, so changed was he by the intersections of his flesh with the building's mutations, existing in both plausible and implausible space.

Bloom Times in Persephone's Limbic System

She didn't risk driving the jeep without them.

High levels of molecular contamination might be exacerbated by Oswald's unconscious aggressions. Though he claimed to value all life equally, from trees to humans to ants, she wondered for the first time: in embracing the specter of human extinction, was he secretly hateful rather than enlightened? What did she really know of him, of his early life and motivations? Could his disordered projections signify anything other than the psychic spewing of a madman's cyst?

She'd return regardless. She had so much to share.

Nursing the first tumor by the side of the road under an overcast sky, Martine had gazed out over the flat plains spanning the empty distances feeling as if an apocalypse had happened centuries ago. Like fragments of some alternate history, the various dooms predicted for humanity had come true and faded from memory with the arduous passage of time. Fire, flood, asteroid crash; an uninhabitable earth was the lone survivor's birthright. Her birthright. Nurturing the mutation fulfilled an embedded genetic contract.

She'd reached the end of the map.

Flip it over and start again, something said.

Awakening in her as she exchanged body fluids with the suckling tumor, this new mind's plasticity seemed to enter her as it kneaded and drank rhythmically.

When more emerged, leaking up through the asphalt in quivering, tentative lumps, in a range of hues from meaty to translucent, a disparity of shapes copious in both breadth and size, their revolting, mutational beauty promised an autonomous, adaptive disease, a life form viable to survive the collapse.

Discovering they required no glands on which to latch, she bared her skin. They grew on her, exchanging cells and depositing lumps inside. She felt the erratic growths proliferating in her body, changing its shape, bringing new imaginings and desires alien to her analytical mind, yet familiar with a fierceness of competitive drive. The irrational idea took root in her, like long lost flesh filling out unmuscled spaces between atoms and bones, that they completed Martine as a perpetuating system resistant to the encroaching void.

The jeep had begun to shift out of sync. She led her brood to its frame. The well-fed growths metastasized into functional schemata, attaching to machinery, fusing unstable parts, and replacing gaps in the vehicle's broken reality with organic, motile, fatty substance. The jeep became more creature than machine.

Working her mutating form onto the seat, Martine laid her hands on the steering wheel. It was slippery with tumors. The gesture was mere habit. She didn't need to steer. The vehicle, now a living biochemical extension of her thoughts, lunged into motion like a large animal and stampeded forward on a vector chosen by Martine's most intrinsic and unknowable self.

At the end was The Castle.

And Oswald waited inside.

Figure at the Endgame of a Crucifixion

Upside-down, twisting through crisscrossing girders, Thorannsson's body intersected radically with the exposed framework of the building. Rebar pierced him. His torso slithered from broken legs, spiraling snake-like down broken concrete to crush his wrecked shoulders. Arms spread out on either side, completing the shape of an inverted cross. His head sat upright at the base, as if the man had been taken apart and put back together wrong.

"Oswald," the head rasped.

Its eyes tracked Teagan's approach.

Closer, the holes where rebar pierced Thorannsson's body were not true wounds but gaps. Within the bleeding slits appeared visible voids in his flesh, small infinities yawning open, swallowing metal rods. Teagan peered inside. Matter disappeared into nothingness, lubricated by blood. Five perforations pulsed and contracted on Thorannsson's torso. They moved with his breath, blinking open and closed, marking the five points of a malleable constellation of fatal injury like a perverse galaxy asking to be explored.

Teagan pushed in five fingers. The holes gave way, soft as tongues.

Thorannsson gasped.

Then he moaned.

"Oswald. Yes."

Sliding deeper, Teagan teased at the void. The surrounding flesh was warm, almost feverish. He brought his fingers together in a fist. Something inside Thorannsson broke. Teagan's arm went numb. An unseen force gripped it. The rest of his body immobilized as if plunged below ice.

Everything went black, although Teagan remained able to see. The blackness was cognitive, like inhabiting an aberrant, deteriorating brain. He knew nothing. Nothing existed. The void smelled of lightning, of all the wires and neurons in the universe burned out. And yet at the same time, it had no smell, no taste, no substance, and no sights to behold.

Nothing but Oswald.

"Please," Teagan said. "Crucify me. Let it end."

The older man hovered intimately close, his lab coat open over a wrinkled button down and a slight paunch. Teagan trembled as Oswald faced him and placed a gentle hand on each shoulder. The warmth and weight of them, the tall aging frame, the deceptively ascetic-looking face nodding patiently, knowingly; and in the glowing timbre of his voice, the man came magically back to life. Teagan's heart broke with joy.

"We have work yet to do," Oswald said. "Not yet."

Hopeless anger burned through Teagan in a flash. Spit flew from his lips. "But I need you more than any of them. Take me. Take everything. Kill me. Kill me."

Oswald's brow furrowed only slightly.

Teagan sobbed and hung his head. "Why must I wait? Why?"

Tears and phlegm streamed from his face. His forehead beat against Oswald's chest. With a practiced, calming hand the back of Teagan's neck, and another encircling the younger man's waist, Oswald pulled Teagan close. He shuddered with rage. He felt he would collapse with grief, but Oswald clasped him tight and held him wordlessly in a long embrace.

Monuments toward a Cathartic Future

The abandoned office park teemed with diseased architecture. From a distance, the chaos of prone, thrusting support beams and interpenetrating deformed cubes assumed the appearance of an orgy among concrete giants.

Martine's jeep lurched quickly like a colony of

disrupted amoebae, tiny in comparison, aimed at the base of the thin black spire rising from the reflecting pond. It spun like crystallized oil, black blades slicing the roar of deconstruction into silence.

The crash was also silent.

Martine rolled out of the jeep as it careened into the eye of the cataleptic void. As if evolving in slow motion, her organic brood extruded the emptiness of the starry gaps and filled it with transitional spaces less hectic. Conscious thought, flickering with the logical stability of death, broke the loop of projections and collapsed myriad pan-directional images into a single and separate endpoint.

The razor tower reversed into a cone folding in on itself. Steel columns stilled against diagonal imperatives. I-beams capitulated. The exposed steel skeletons of the buildings hardened into normalcy. Floors and walls ceased bending and funneling into a visual nonsense of disassociated angles. Rooms settled into approximate square.

Although evidence of catastrophe surrounded her, Martine's gamble had worked. The buildings were still. Oswald's uncontrolled projections would, she hoped, remain locked away, far from reality, silenced and safe. She only had to find him in the rubble.

Who by Avalanche, Who by Powder

Thorannsson was dead. The corpse made a wet, gaseous sound as he pulled his fist out of it. The impalements were not his doing, but pedestrian ethical qualms didn't prevent him making use of them. All things being equal, nature abhorred a waste. Utilitarianism was environmentally sound and thus sufficiently respectful to the dead.

He patted the pockets of his lab coat with the distinct sensation that he'd lost something, smearing it with corpse fluids. Certainly some time was missing, but that wasn't unusual.

Perhaps the complexity of the architectural malady had confused him, or maybe he'd forgotten another interminable meeting with some minor biologist on staff. One of the few benefits of his age was the excuse it gave him for dodging such tiresome and mundane tasks. The young people didn't question his demands for privacy or rest. They must think him infirm.

Martine could tell them a thing or two, he chuckled. Although truth be told, he was growing bored with her. He'd suggest a threesome soon; see if she was amenable—or had they already done that? Was there a sound like another man's voice in is head, or had he simply dreamed the young, attractive guardian angel who seduced him and laid him down to sleep as the world collapsed?

"Oswald," said Martine, appearing as if summoned by his thoughts. She gestured at his soiled lab coat, eyebrow raised in a chastising flirt. "I knew I'd find you up to no good."

That couldn't be right. He was mixed up, had forgotten something important. He was about to ask for clarification when she kissed him.

Then she stood back, and she was smiling. She was mutating. Her disheveled appearance coupled with the erotic possibilities suggested by the burgeoning lumps that swelled beneath her skin and adhered like tumescent sex organs on the outside of her flesh excited him. He grabbed her by the throat, caressing the wet lumps that writhed all the way down to her navel and made her bulge with new curves, kissing and pressing his teeth into the soft places, dropping to his knees to explore her evolving shape. Martine grew large above him and gasped with a colony of need.

Elsewhere, nowhere, trapped in a void of abject silence on the empty stage set of a madman's coma, burning with repressed rage and impossible desire, Teagan writhed at the base of an abstract crucifixion and screamed his soundless plea: *Kill me. Kill me.*

Farewell to the Mycelium
Brendan Vidito

Rowan Meldrum—disgraced psychiatrist turned black market neurosurgeon—operated from the basement of a ramen shop in the bowels of the city. The building was an abscess on a landscape of ruin and dilapidation, its blackened brick twice darkened by the shadows of looming megastructures. A cat's cradle of ancient electrical wire sagged overhead, supported by a line of rotten wooden poles. These relics were only found in neighbourhoods long forsaken by civic authorities and had come to serve as bellwethers heralding danger and disorder. The stench of raw sewage rose from the street, which was darker than the sky. A glowing, red lantern in the shop window provided the sole illumination. And it was this light—this beacon—that guided Blythe Travers toward the renegade doctor, on a search to find a cure for his madness.

A bell chimed as Travers shouldered his way into the shop. The abrupt change in atmosphere overwhelmed his already overwrought senses. Notes of rich simmering broth, aromatic oils, garlic, ginger, and braised pork filled the air. Everywhere he looked: garish Japanese décor in red and gold and ochre. Paper lanterns hung from the low, beamed ceiling. And a *maneki-neko*, perched on a dais in the entrance, beckoned him with a languid, pendulous paw. The place proved to be even more stimulating than his long journey through the leprous undercity.

As he continued to scan his environment—quick, nervous, almost rabbit-like—a volley of pop-ups circumvented his defence parameters. He nearly cried out. A personal advert for Asian singles intruded on his line of sight—the woman airbrushed and clad only in lacy black underwear. Beside it, a roulette wheel spun and flashed in an obnoxious kaleidoscope. Below, a fraudulent error message stated his cerebrospinal fluid was compromised. The restaurant had all but disappeared behind this veil of nonsense. Travers closed his eyes and performed a soft reset, embarrassed by his reaction. He shouldn't have been surprised by the intrusion. The more lawless sectors of the city were a breeding ground for spam and malicious hyphal signals. When he opened his eyes, his vision had cleared, and he approached the counter.

An employee emerged from behind a curtain and greeted him with a bow. A link to the menu appeared in his peripherals, but he ignored it. He felt a twinge as his personal information travelled along the Mycelial Network and entered this stranger's mind. At the same time, her personal history came to him in a flash of insight. Midori Kimura. Age thirty-seven. Widowed. Two children. Immigrated from Fukuoka seven years ago. Spoke Japanese and English. Spent most of her non-working hours tending to her children and watching immersive soap operas. She currently suffered from a yeast infection.

They shared an awkward smile.

"How can I help you, Mr. Travers?"

As with most of his interactions, Travers marvelled at the woman's stillness. She appeared unaffected by the endless streams of information vying for attention inside her skull. News bulletins. Subjective observations from friends and strangers alike. Curated advertisements. Decrypted records of her biological processes. New and novel forms of art and media. Voices upon voices upon voices. And yet, she was perfectly adapted to the onslaught. Mind and body calibrated with the organized chaos of the Mycelial feed.

Travers, on the other hand, was a mess of tics, blinks and twitches. Chronic stress had whittled him down into a gaunt, pale, subhuman thing. He was perpetually distracted, ill-kempt, and cursed by the fearful, panic-stricken mind of a prey animal.

He leaned across the counter, unsure whether this conspiratorial gesture was needed, and said, "I—I'd like to speak with Doctor Meldrum. I heard he runs a practice here."

She laughed. It was coarser than he would have expected. "A practice," she said, her tone mocking. "Give me your hand."

"I'm sorry?"

"Your hand," she gestured, impatient.

Travers placed his hand—riddled with tremors—palm down on the counter. Midori grabbed it—her fingers bony and cold—and squeezed. He knew what she was planning before he felt the fibres penetrate his skin. Within seconds, they were linked, network to network, one digital soul to another. A union more intimate than raw intercourse. And like that unprotected act, the transmission of contagion was a real possibility. Travers sensed something—a subharmonic whisper—travel along the fibres threading his nerve endings. He tried to pull away, but she held fast. His vision glitched. He tasted metal. Panic bloomed and threatened to overtake him. But before he could voice his alarm, Midori released his hand and cast it away like a venomous reptile.

"You're clear," she said.

Travers cradled his hand against his chest. "What did you do?"

"Had to make sure you weren't affiliated with law enforcement." She squirted hand sanitizer from a dispenser on the counter into her palm and worked it between her fingers. "And I installed a minor blackout program. Everything you see here—until you leave the building that is—will be wiped from your archives. No one will know you were here."

Travers relaxed. "Yes, okay. And the, uh, doctor?"

"Next to the bathroom. Take the stairs."

MELDRUM SAT on a foldout chair in the corner of the basement, a bowl of noodles between his knees. Chopsticks dangled from his mouth as he read from a paperback—an actual physical book bound with paper and glue Travers had only ever seen in museums. He wore a button-down disco shirt, but no pants. His underwear was just visible below the hem of the shirt. All around him stood shelves of medical and electronic equipment. And in the middle of the room, an operating chair—gleaming steel and leather beneath an extinguished surgical light.

When he noticed Travers, he jumped, and the chopsticks clattered to the floor.

"Christ," he said. "Who are you?"

Travers looked on in confusion. "What do you mean? You can't see my information?" he said, alluding to the Mycelial communion that occurred whenever two people came into contact. Before Meldrum could answer, though, Travers realized he wasn't receiving the man's personal history, either. In fact, the Mycelium was unusually quiet. For once, his mind was empty of all save his own thoughts. It was the silence he craved—the long-sought remedy to his madness.

Meldrum waved an arm around the room. "The place is rigged with agonists that dampen the bioelectrical impulses of the Mycelium. Down here, I don't want anyone peering into my head, and I don't care to see what kind of perversions lurk in the minds of my patients." He set his book and noodles on a shelf. Picked his pants off the floor and slid them on. "So, I'll ask you again. Who are you?"

"My name is Blythe Travers. I—"

"Why are you here so late?"

"I work during the day. And it took me longer than I hoped to find the place."

Meldrum burped. "You run into any trouble?"

"Not really."

"What does that mean?"

"I ran into some derelicts. They challenged me, but lost interest and let me alone."

With a knowing nod, Meldrum said, "This part of the city is teeming with them. They've formed something of a colony in the abandoned megastructures. A hive of the lost." He paced the room and found a half-empty bottle of electrolyte juice, downed it in one swallow. "They will be the inheritors of a new society when everything else inevitably collapses in on itself. And good for them." He tossed the empty bottle across the room, aiming for the trash can, but missing by inches. "Now, what can I help you with?"

Travers took a deep breath. "I want you to sever me from the Mycelium."

Meldrum arched his brow. "That is rather extreme."

"Have you done it before?"

"Yes, but it's far from a common procedure. Humans are social creatures, after all. They enjoy the connection. What are you, a misanthrope?" He dragged and unfolded a second chair that leaned against the wall. Gestured for Travers to take a seat. He did. Meldrum carried his chair over and sat opposite his patient, leaning forward, hands dangling between his knees.

"No, that's not why I'm here." Travers paused to consider his words. "I think the Mycelium is making me sick. Here, I mean," and he pointed at his temple. "I can't stand the constant reams of information. The bombardments of collective neural impulses. I'm not like most people. I can't integrate the Mycelium into my life. It's slowly killing me. I've turned to drugs like ThinkDeath, but they're not working. Or they're not strong enough." He took a deep, tremulous breath. "There's too many voices in my head."

Meldrum nodded. A faint smile etched on his lips.

"You want some good old-fashioned peace and quiet."

"Yes," Travers said. "Like this." He breathed out, weary but serene, and motioned with his chin to the silent walls around them.

Meldrum straightened. "Unfortunately for you, this technology is not easily replicated. It's also highly illegal and wouldn't solve your problem in the long term."

"Surgery, then?"

"Perhaps." He crossed his arms. "You know, there was a time—long ago—when voices in the mind were considered a symptom of madness. And before that, an omen of demonic influence. Now everyone has a plethora of voices inside them, some conflicting, idiotic, brilliant. Others hateful, misleading, reasonable, or fatalistic. It makes you wonder, with so many voices swirling around our skulls, can we continue to call our minds our own? Or is our every thought and feeling a product mass-produced by the interconnection of the Mycelium?"

"I never thought of it that way before." Travers said. "You don't seem to have a high opinion of the Mycelium."

He shrugged. "Humanity is flawed, so everything we create will carry that stain of imperfection. Some creations, though, are greater blunders than others. My personal research has led me to one conclusion. The Mycelium—however heretical it might be to point out —is unnatural to the human mind. Its creators believed in a link between our early ancestors, the dawn of consciousness, and the mind-altering properties of psychogenic mushrooms. They sought to replicate that evolutionary leap by injecting spores infused with information straight into our brains. It altered us in a fundamental way, but it may not have been for the better. In fact, it might have been downright irresponsible."

"All I know is I want to be healed of this madness."

Meldrum held up a finger. "I don't believe you've been experiencing madness. Or, at least, *you* are not mad. Quite the contrary. I think you're saner than you can possibly know. The Mycelium itself, on the other hand, *is* madness. A shared schizophrenia that alters our perception of reality and undermines our intellectual capacity."

"Does that mean you'll help me?"

"Yes, Blythe, I will help you."

"I have the money."

He reached into his pocket and removed a spore capsule infused with fifty thousand units. The amount recorded on the price board of an illegal marketplace deep in the ungoverned depths of the Mycelial subconscious. For Travers, it was over a year's salary.

"I know." The doctor pocketed the capsule. "You wouldn't be here otherwise."

"Is it dangerous?"

"It's a delicate procedure. Your chances of dying aren't zero."

"What are the risks?"

"Short-term memory loss, synaesthesia, chronic nerve pain, seizures, colorblindness, loss of taste or smell, involuntary movements, narcolepsy, hypnagogic hallucinations—"

"What's that?"

"Waking dreams."

"The list goes on."

"There are plenty of potential side effects. But they're rare. The success rate for this procedure is usually high. No one has died in my chair yet."

"Hopefully I'm not the first."

Meldrum grinned and clapped Travers on the shoulder. After a moment, his features hardened into a grim mask of apprehension. He said, "You must understand that your life will not be the same after you wake from surgery. You will be alienated from the rest of humanity. Divested of the conveniences of the Mycelium. You will have to learn to work around the societal barriers in place for those who are not connected. It will be a slow, painful, and most all, lonely process. I want to know that you acknowledge these challenges before we proceed."

Travers had exhausted a lifetime of misery struggling against an adversary he could not hope to overcome. Now, his salvation was at hand, and he could think of no other alternative than the bite of the surgeon's knife. No matter how arduous the aftermath, its hidden possibilities and the rare chance of a tabula rasa, far surpassed the existence he would leave behind. He was more than prepared for the challenges. He would embrace them.

"I understand," he said. "And I'm ready."

"All right, then. Let's begin."

Light pried at his eyelids. His skull throbbed. All the moisture in his mouth had disappeared and his tongue was swollen, thinning the air in his lungs. He inhaled through blood-caked nostrils. The air stank, a sour garbage smell. He shifted and something sharp bit into his shoulder blade. He repositioned his body again and soft tendrils fell across his forehead. He brushed them away, but they returned almost immediately, irritating the bridge of his nose. Awareness continued to dawn in increments until he managed to open his eyes.

A leaden sky. Carrion birds wheeling high overhead.

His mind was silent except for the heavy drum of his headache.

No Mycelial chatter. No intrusive visuals. The voices were gone.

Travers sat up with a groan. He'd been lying in a pile of refuse, sprawled among used takeout containers, broken glass, soiled condoms and bloated, ruptured bin bags. His shoes and socks were missing. The tendrils he'd noticed earlier swept into his eyes and, irritated, he tried to remove their source from upon his head, only to realize they were a fringe of his own hair—now grown longer than he remembered it. A wave of dizziness crashed through him as he lost all sense of time. What lay in the murk between his anesthetization and awakening? And why had the doctor abandoned him here of all places? Was he unloaded somewhere else and carried here by a third party? Like a group of derelicts? Meldrum's inheritors of the new world. None of this made any sense, but his knowledge that the procedure had been a success eclipsed any lingering confusion. His lifetime of torment was at an end, and all he wanted now was a warm shower and to bask in the silence of his apartment.

Slow, unsteady, he rose to his feet. The world swam and he almost lost his balance. He slapped a hand to his forehead and moaned through gritted teeth. *You can do this*, he thought. *Take it easy.* He stepped through debris, careful not to lacerate his feet. Once clear of the garbage pile, he took stock of his surroundings. A wide, ruined street. On either side, colossal warehouses reared their sinister black walls against the late-morning sunlight. There were no sidewalks, no people, and every sign had been uprooted from the concrete. This part of the city was just as deserted during the day as it was at night. It recalled the imminent collapse Meldrum had prophesied. With a halting stride, Travers began to walk toward the city centre.

A block or so later, a restored sense of stability invigorated his stride. The headache receded to a dull ache. And he came to recognize that his senses—in the absence of the Mycelium—were sharpened. Colours—though scarce here—were brighter, more vibrant.

There was a depth of richness in the breeze, the pungence of industry, the hint of brine from the coast. He registered every pebble and grain on the soles of his feet. His shirt sighed against his skin as he walked. The world felt alive for the first time he could remember. He walked on and let his emotions pour forth.

AFTER A TIME, Travers entered a liminal region known as The Slope. A slow ascending grade between the decay of the undercity and the city centre with its commerce and tides of commuters. The buildings here were fewer, but in good repair. Delivery drones ferried cargo between the sectors, gliding—noiseless—along the road, or several meters overhead. A scant few trees grew here, preserved like amber in their prisons of glass. Travers approached one of them, eyes aflame with wonder. The leaves were much greener than he remembered, their surfaces gleaming like polished leather. The bark, with its intricate whorls and ridges, drew his gaze until he was unable to look away. His mind conjured a litany of praise for this newfound beauty. And, for once, his internal musings weren't overwhelmed and snuffed out by the collective barrage. He could linger on every word, every flitting observation. The freedom was awe-inspiring. He felt like a prisoner released from a lifetime of confinement.

When his devotions were complete, Travers continued up The Slope. He didn't venture far before stopping again. This time not in a state of rapture, but bewilderment.

A person stood on the sidewalk ahead, motionless, their back to him, head tilted to the sky. They wore a sweater, the sleeves rolled up above the elbows, and black trousers. Their hair didn't move with the wind. The strands were instead flattened and fused to the scalp. Mannequin hair. The skin was stranger still. White as spun silk and as textured as fibreglass. It caught and reflected the sunlight, making it appear as though it were glowing.

Frowning, Travers approached. "Excuse me."

No response.

He walked around until he faced the figure. His stomach fell. The face was rigid, lifeless. Eyes open but textured like the fiberglass skin. Only glossier. The irises a weave of greenish gold fibers. The nose was nothing more than a cavity. And the mouth, with its pink-shaded lips, was open enough to glimpse a row of realistic and unsettling human-like teeth. A dummy or bizarre art project of some kind. But why was it here? In the middle of the sidewalk of the underpopulated Slope? Was it dropped by one of the delivery drones?

He reached out to touch it, but before making contact, a sound issued from the anomaly, and he pulled away. A slow, whining susurrus—part cockroach hiss, part audio feedback. Travers took a step back, then another. A hidden speaker? Wind passing through the fibres to produce the sound? For a brief, guilty moment he wished he could consult the Mycelium for answers. But lacking that ability, he had no choice but to let this mystery remain an open question. Reluctant and uneasy, he gave the mannequin a parting glance before he started toward a tunnel that led to the city centre.

LIGHT, mirrored from the jagged peaks of commercial megastructures, stunned Travers as he emerged from the dusk of the tunnel. The city, an amalgam of glass and chrome and kinetic billboards, exploded into his field of view. As his vision adjusted to the glare, and his ears tuned to the sudden influx of noise, he realized something was deeply and fundamentally wrong.

A familiar hissing whine replaced the discordant hum of human voices. And the ebb and flow of pedestrian traffic—a daily sight for Travers—was controverted by an uncanny stillness. There were people everywhere he looked, but none of them were moving.

He approached the nearest individual, a woman frozen under a streetlamp. Her skin was corpse white and threaded like fiberglass. Travers choked back a scream. In a panic, he raced to a cluster of commuters a few paces away. More of the same. Their lustrous, woven eyes stared ahead, locked in their sockets. He turned. Three more grinned at him with teeth too real for their artificial bodies. Another turn. This time pulling something in his neck. A dozen more mannequins were frozen midstride, aimed in his direction. Staring. Grinning.

What the fuck was going on? Was this a side effect of the procedure? He tried to rhyme off the potential risks in his head. Short-term memory loss. Seizures. Colorblindness. What was the last one again? Hypnasomething. Waking dreams. Did that explain these mannequins? Were they real people and he was hallucinating them as lifeless effigies? How did that even make any sense? Why weren't they moving? Why couldn't he hear them speaking? Maybe they weren't real people, but something else. But then, where were all the people? Maybe he was still asleep in the doctor's chair, in the grip of a nightmare. *What do I do? What the fuck do I do?*

He spun around again, trembling, breathing hard, and his shoulder collided with a male mannequin. It teetered, hung balanced for a second, then tipped onto its side. The whining hiss all around him flared to a deafening pitch. And, in amongst the din, Travers sensed notes of shock and accusation. He clapped his hands over his ears, and the scream he had been holding back finally exploded from his throat. All he could think to do was run.

He did so haphazardly, blinded by panic. Inanimate faces flashed across his vision with every stride. Wide staring eyes. Those realistic teeth. He couldn't escape them. He ran. And ran until his lungs burned and his feet were bleeding. When he couldn't run anymore, he leaned against a pillar and vomited until nothing but saliva strung from his lips. Groaning, he looked up. He had somehow managed to flee onto a subway platform. The place teemed with mannequins; their unnatural pallor accentuated under the blue, bioluminescent fixtures. The train glided without a sound from the mouth of the tunnel, stopped and opened its doors. None embarked, none emerged. A minute later, the doors closed, and the train disappeared down the tunnel. All was silent save the low susurrus of the mannequins.

"Meldrum," Travers croaked, once his mind was calm. "I need to see the doctor."

Perhaps there was a chance he was unaffected by this phenomenon.

He wiped his mouth on the sleeve of his shirt and

stood up straight. He started to walk back, toward The Slope, but his feet were so bloodied and torn, he could only manage a plodding limp. This wouldn't work. He needed to dress the wounds, protect his feet. He faced the subway platform again, looked down at the shoes on the nearest mannequin. Brown loafers. He approached and measured his foot against them. A size or two bigger than his own, but that was for the best. He needed room for makeshift bandages. He pushed the mannequin over, eliciting a choir of hissing protestations. Bending over he removed the shoes and socks. He then made his way to the head of the mannequin and removed its shirt. He tore the white fabric into strips and wrapped them around his feet. He pulled on the socks and carefully slid into the shoes. The pain was still present but muted by the cushion of the bandages. He headed toward the street again, and by the time he reached the tunnel, the sun was already in decline. He wouldn't reach the undercity until nightfall. But he had no other choice. If one person could end this nightmare, it was Rowan Meldrum.

NIGHT LAY thick over the vicinity of the ramen shop. The red lantern in the window shone like a cycloptic eye through the blackness, watching as Travers limped and stumbled toward the front door. He pushed his way inside, almost losing his balance and spilling, face-first, to the floor. Behind the counter, Midori stood stock-still, pale and staring. The likeness was striking, and that much more unsettling because of it. Her unnatural flesh was obscene against the craftsmanship of her kimono. As Travers moved passed her, toward the basement door, a susurrating buzz filled the room. A protestation in a language he could not discern. He paid it no heed and took the stairs.

With each step, he prayed, pleaded with any higher power who would listen, that he would reach the bottom and find a living, breathing man. Anything less and he was doomed. As he neared the final stair, he slowed, slivers of doubt pushing through him, flickering the hope already dimming in his mind. He closed his eyes as he reached the concrete floor and waited to hear the doctor's voice. Instead, he was greeted with nothing but silence. He opened his eyes. And voiced an animal howl of despair. The mannequin doctor stood in the corner of the room, facing one of the many shelves.

"Meldrum," Travers screamed.

The now familiar hissing rose in answer, though it was quieter than on previous occasions. Were the agonists installed in the room working on the sound?

Dampening its range in the same way they muted the powers of the Mycelium? Were the two—the mannequins and the Mycelium— somehow connected? Separate pieces of a singular madness.

Travers stormed toward to the doctor. Grabbed him. Spun him around. The mannequins could not replicate the wrinkles on the human face, and so Meldrum looked ten years younger. He stared into Travers, blue eyes glistening. His mouth was opened slightly as though in protest. Travers slammed the Meldrum-mannequin against the shelf. Medical packets and computer chips rained to the floor. Its body was lighter than it would have been in life. Not hollow. But the mass was focused to a singular point inside the torso. The limbs and head, though, seemed empty, or else made of the same lightweight material as the skin.

"Can you hear me?" Travers said. "I need your help."

The susurrations took on a fluctuant character.

"Something went wrong with the procedure."

The Meldrum-mannequin stared. And Travers slammed it against the shelf again.

"There's something wrong with my perception."

Still nothing. But did he really expect an answer?

The volume drained from his voice. "I need to know if I'll be okay."

Then, through the hiss and static, came a whisper, the insinuation of speech. Travers leaned in, ear to the mannequin's mouth, and listened. *You. Were. Dead.* The voice was undeniably Meldrum's but drained of volume and timbre. The voice of a ghost.

"Dead?" Travers said. "What do you mean? Did I die on the table?"

Silence from the mannequin, not even the usual susurrations.

"Answer me."

Still nothing.

Travers heaved a tremulous breath. If he had died in the operating chair, that would explain why he woke on a pile in garbage in a derelict part of the undercity. Meldrum had disposed of his corpse. But it had been a mistake. It had to be. How else would he walking around right now?

"Meldrum," he said. "What do you mean *dead*?"

The mannequin was silent.

"Fuck you. Answer me."

Slam.

"Answer me."

Slam. Slam.

"You need to help me."

Slam. Slam. Slam. Slam. SLAM.

"You need to help—"

A dry crack echoed throughout the basement.

Travers froze. A smell like a butcher's table rose to his nostrils, and he gagged. He staggered backward and released the Meldrum-mannequin. It fell against the shelf and toppled sideways, bending unnaturally as it struck the floor.

Sick with dread, Travers looked down.

The violence of his interrogation had severed the mannequin at the waist. A jagged fracture ran from hip to armpit. And spilling from the interior was a mass of organs, slick, musty and still twitching with an unspeakable form of life. They oozed across the floor, carried on a growing pool of blood, brighter, more vivid and more real than any blood ought to be from within the shell of an artificial construct. Travers ran screaming from the building.

THE DERELICT WOKE as the sun reddened outside the penthouse window. He rubbed his eyes and inspected the space beside his sleeping bag. Three cans of vegetables. A tube of toothpaste. And a pair of vacuum-sealed sandwiches. His benefactors had once again visited him during the night. He had never seen them, though he assumed they too were homeless. They moved in the depths of his unconsciousness, like fairy-folk in a fable. But even if he managed to catch a glimpse of them, he doubted he would see flesh and blood. Rather, they would appear to him as inanimate figures woven from countless Mycelial fibres. The new sapiens of this interconnected world. And for this reason, their nocturnal deliveries were a blessing.

He scratched his beard and tore open one of the sandwiches. As he ate, he moved to the window. His lodgings were located at the zenith of the abandoned megastructure. The clouds shuttled close overhead, stained pink from the setting sun. Two thousand feet below, the undercity festered in darkness. And further distant, the city centre glowed with galactic fervour. From this vantage, the derelict knew only silence and solitude. These elements constituted his world. One thought only carried him from one day to the next. A prophecy told by a man he had known long ago. A man he had murdered. The inhabitants of the undercity, this man had prophesied, would be the inheritors of a new society when the old inevitably collapsed. The derelict held onto these words and waited with bated breath for the skies to open and the world to begin anew.

Fractal Decay

Donyae Coles

Suchansuch had never left the City.

She remembered her first day there, sort of, in the hazy half dream way of something long ago but she remembered more that she'd never left it at all. She remembered more the way the City sparkled, all bright lights and advertisements. Wide, golden shop windows, plastic bodies draped in finery, beckoning. The deep, velvet dark bars, smoke dancing, sweet liquor promises calling.

Everything so welcoming and wanting like Suchansuch was welcoming and wanting.

She had come to the City and she had always been in the City.

TeeVee leaned back on the settee, naked, legs spread showing everything there was to show, the light playing off all of her soft, honey curves. Her dark green braids, installed for this session, were spilling all over the velvet cushions, hiding nothing.

They paid three quarters of their income to keep the roof over their heads, to stay inside the white-washed walls where Suchandsuch stacked her canvas to dry. A single bedroom, a living room that she used as a studio, half a kitchen and a bathroom with no tub. Every room was decorated with traces of them. It smelled of linseed oil and sparkled with bits and pieces of costumes. In the summer it was dripping rainforest jungle hot and in the winter it was nose bleed dry desert hot. They had no control of the heat, they didn't think the central air, promised for three quarters of their income, was real.

But they were real. In the heat of summer, the heat of winter, they tangled in each other's arms and legs, buried fingers and tongues in each other. They'd met at a bar, setting up a show. Such had been invited to hang her art, hoped to sell a few pieces to make rent on what had been then her little room in a shared three-bedroom spot in a building that rumbled and swayed when a truck passed.

TeeVee was there to dance, part of the real show, the ticket drawer. Such was there in hopes that someone would notice her paintings, would desire them as much as she desired TeeVee. The dancer wore a loose crop top and high cut shorts, bare feet. Her skin glowed red gold under the stage lights. Her braids, adorned with silver beads shot diamonds through the air with each spin.

Suchandsuch would have watched her for hours but the paintings needed hung if they were going to be seen. And she was just a dull thing, small and brown and soft like a finch. Her paintings were the interesting thing, and she their quiet creator. They were in different orbits.

But TeeVee came before the show when Such placed the last bits of her soul on the wall. Empty alleys covered in glistening garbage, portraits of the friends she'd made in smeared after-party makeup when they were their softest and most beautiful.

"You need some color too," TeeVee said, bending, and pressing her lipstick adorned lips to Such's, blessing her with a shock of candy red. "There," TeeVee said, pulling back, all smiles, the sky's missing stars in her eyes, "Now you match your art."

Such returned her gift after the show. She took a photo of her own face in the early morning hazy dawn light of the city. Eyes wide, shocked, brown skin dressed in red lip shaped blooms, her own mouth slightly parted and swollen.

She painted the selfie, it was the only time she'd felt beautiful in her life. She moved in with TeeVee, into the apartment that ate their money three weeks later and TeeVee hung it in their little living room/studio, all the people and places she painted, spiraling around her.

"You ever been anywhere?" Such asked licking salt sweat from the space between TeeVee's breasts on their first night together in their new place. No curtains, the light of the billboard across from the window bathed them in red light. The bank they both used, the advertising wasted on them.

"Sure, we've all been places," she said sighing and then there was no more room for questions and wonderings.

In the City they found each other. TeeVee the dancer. Suchandsuch the artist. In the City they were *something* and they both, dreamlike deep memory, remembered not being anything, so they paid thee quarters of their wages to have a place. They danced and sold paintings in between serving coffee and hanging shirts to make it a home under the never dark and endless sky.

Such worked at her canvas recreating her lover in soft tones, made her a witch, made her apartment the sea. She had never seen the sea. She had never left the City. None of them had left the City.

But she dreamed about it, the sea. She dreamed in oil and acrylic about the wide world that existed beyond the concrete and steel and glass. The stars somewhere above the lights. The rivers that had never seen a road. But she had never left the City.

No one left the City.

"I need a break," TeeVee sang from the seat.

"I've got it blocked out, go head, I'll keep working," Such replied, not looking up, absorbed by the work. An artist, a brave thing to be outside of the City but inside its hot walls, everyone was an artist or a poet or a musician or they were nothing at all.

She finally looked up, looked away from the canvas, the dream in oil, to the shabby real world beyond and there was no one there.

"Vee?" she called to the little apartment. Looked behind her to the half a kitchen cast in orange light. Put down her brush and crossed the worn, gray carpet to the bedroom door. Opening it found nothing but their bed bathed in red glow from the electric billboard. "Vee?" she called again, anyway.

The bathroom was empty. The apartment was empty. Just Such and her paintings.

It was like TeeVee had never been there at all. Her makeup, her clothing, the bits of mess from used dishes and discarded tissues all missing and only Such's sparse existence still habiting the too small too expensive place. The only thing left of TeeVee was the vision of her on the easel, unfinished yet but there.

Real.

Her face, lips turned in a coy smile, the silver-gray couch under her wide opened limbs. And beyond her, done in quick slashes was a black void, a note to paint in later with something. TeeVee said it should be her, should be Such, they were together but Such refused. She was the artist.

The low rumble of worry started in Such's belly and she ignored it. TeeVee said she needed a break, probably went for a walk. Such, dabs of paint all over her smock dress giving her strange plumage, slid her feet into a pair of sandals. Grabbed keys and phone and small backpack. Left the little apartment that ate up too much of their too little money.

The hallway was a wall of heat. Dim light, identical closed doors. It smelled like cabbage and piss. Such walked down the four stories to the ground floor and out into the City night. Breathed in concrete and exhaust and called it fresh.

"Hey, Such!" Lady called from across the street. An old woman, she used to dance like TeeVee danced but now she just sat at her window, watched. Spread gossip that sounded like warnings. Sometimes she sat on the stoop, like she sat then, enjoyed the cooler night in the summer. Like they all did because the promised air conditioning never seemed to work for any of them. "You sell any of them paintings you're always doing? I saw you putting all them big ones in the that van the other day."

The night was alive, people laughing, drinking. Kids up a little too late. The City in summer.

"Hey!" Such waved back. "You mean for the show downtown. Yeah actually! Sold *King of Dawn.* You know, I showed you that one. With Leonard."

The old woman nodded in that way that old people do when they don't remember but they're still proud of you. Still happy for you. "That's good. That's good."

Such nodded back, then, "Have you seen TeeVee? I think she left but she didn't say anything."

Lady shook her head. "I just got out here. Too damn hot up there," she said thumbing back to her window."

"Alright, thanks, she probably just walked down to the corner," Such said, shrugging.

"You know, you get used to it, in the City. Been here as long as me, you get used to it," Lady said waving a paper fan over her wrinkled face and chest.

Such paused, mid-step. Her tone was low and sad. *Heavy.* It wasn't the heat even though that's what Suchandsuch wanted to say, didn't want to ask anything, just wanted to go because she needed to find TeeVee. "Get used to what?"

"To living with a used-to-be. You stay here long enough and everything will be a used-to-be," Lady said looking down the street, towards the corner store. "That place's had eight owners, ten different names in twenty years. You know what twenty years feels like?"

Such smiled, laughed a little. "Yeah, I've made it at least that far."

"Then you don't know. Living for twenty years isn't the same as living through twenty years."

"Then what's it feel like?" Such asked.

Lady fanned herself, turned back to Such. "Feels like yesterday. Feels like you don't even know anymore. Go on head, before you miss her," Lady said, finishing the conversation.

Such waved walked down the street. To the corner store of ten different names. It was Murry's when they moved into the apartment. It was Stop N Shop now. It still had all the same products. Prepackaged sandwiches, chips, and snack cakes. Cans of soda, bottles of juice. Some sad produce that no one ever purchased and always seemed to be at the same not quite rotten stage of its lifecycle. Hanging at the edge of forever.

A couple walked past, holding hands. She didn't know them. They saw only each other, under the streetlight, their skin glowed. Two steps and she thought to look back, that they looked like art but there was no one there.

The light flickered, popped. The sidewalk became pond of darkness between two poles. It moved like water, silky, lapping at the edges of the orange lamps. A sudden rupture in the concreate of the street, darker than asphalt, the sky above. Such shook her head at it, focused on what she'd missed, what she was missing because the space between lights was so hard to look at. Upset at not thinking faster, capturing the moment better. It would have been a lovely thing in oil. She had to find TeeVee.

Such turned away, started back down the block, past the run down but still livable, after all, they were still living in them, buildings that made up her neighborhood. A cacophony of styles, built, burned down, refinished, repainted. Unique enough in their own ways. Inside a few windows glittered but most were dark spaces.

The rents were rising. The cost of living was rising. It was everywhere but it was the rent mostly. She ignored the for-sale signs plastered over with sold stickers. She ignored the lack of laughter in the summer night heat. How empty and quiet the street was. It was late but the City was always open.

There was always somewhere to go in the City.

A bus rumbled past, dark inside, its shift over, heading back to the depot where it would wait until morning to start all over again. Such walked the last half block to the corner. The bell jingled as the door opened. The light changed from orange warmth to cool blue fluorescent that covered everything like snow.

The shelves were packed full of packaged goods. Red and blue printed clear cellophane dominated between spots of yellow. Primary colors. The freezers in the back glowed and hummed with lukewarm soda promises.

Young teen laughter bubbled up, found its way to her from across the shelves. Disembodied, she couldn't find the source. Such stepped into the store, looked around for someone, anyone.

Behind the counter sat a bored twenty something. Acne scars across her cheeks like freckles over her bronze skin. Her hair was in tight braids against her skull, chin resting in her palm, fingers topped with dagger nails, she stared at nothing. Such should know her, they, she and TeeVee came in all the time. Early morning half-drunk before collapsing into bed, evening bored and in need of something, anything to snack on. To consume and feel full. She should know her but she doesn't.

"Hey! Did you see a lady with green braids come in here?" Such asked

Her eyes moved, flicked up and down and then back to nothing. Such turned to see what held her attention.

The door. The world was a black hole beyond.

"She didn't buy nothing," the counter girl said.

Such couldn't figure out if that meant a yes or a no to her question. If she'd come in or not. "So, did you see her?"

"She didn't buy nothing," she repeated. She turned her eyes, bored, sleepy eyes, back to Such. "Can I help you?"

"Guess not," Such sighed. She'd missed her, TeeVee.

The counter girl turned back to the door. Such slipped into the back of the store, where the freezers sat, not cold but lit up, waiting. The teens laughed in that way that sounded like it was about her, that *not part of the joke* way. She turned around to see the door closing, bell swinging and singing. Missed them but the counter girl had seen, her gaze stuck to the door.

Such turned back to the bright world of the freezer. Opened it and was hit with the cooler but not cool enough air of the dying appliance. She scanned over the offerings, picked the one she thought would taste best lukewarm.

"Hey, Such!"

"Leonard!" she sang, like a bell, turning to the voice. Tall, thick man, curly, reddish hair shorn short over light brown skin. The man from the painting she'd sold. Only it wasn't him, not really. It was an aspect of him, done up and transformed as she had transformed TeeVee. He held his arms open, accepted her hug.

"What are you doing out tonight."

"Looking for TeeVee. We were working on a painting. She said she needed a break and I thought she came down for a snack but she's not here."

"Maybe she went over to Leona's. They're having a blackout party."

"Maybe, but she didn't say anything. She'd say something before she went, wouldn't she?"

He shrugged. "You know how she is. You try calling her?" he laughed. "You didn't! You artists. I bet she did go to that party."

Such took out her phone to look away. So simple, why didn't she think about it. No missed calls but no signal either. "It's the store. It's like the walls are made from lead in here," she laughed.

There was a text message. From Leona. About the blackout party.

Hey hey hey there's no power! Bring candles and food!

No more information needed. Someone would bring music. Someone would string battery powered fairy lights. Someone would keep them all going. And TeeVee probably went. Probably expected to see her wander over there as soon as she broke free from the painting and realized that she was alone.

"You going?" she asked, looking up at Leonard's wide face.

He shook his head. "I'm not taking public transportation! Already too damn hot." He reached behind him, came back with a pack of six white, emergency candles. Small, the length of a finger. "Here take these. I'll pay for them, say they were from me."

"Maybe we can call a cab, it's not far," she tried. "I sold your painting. I texted you about it! I can afford the ride."

"Then I'll live forever," he said. "Save your money. Get going before you miss her."

Such paused, déjà vu creeping over her. The same thing that Lady had said. Same tone.

He smiled then, huge grin, beautiful. Leonard who lived half a block away. Who'd they met dancing one night and split a cab home with. Leonard who she'd painted a portrait of in her little living room studio, posed like a king in leather. Sweat poured from him and she made it glitter on canvas. Leonard whose painting had been bought for more money than she'd ever seen at once by someone she'd never seen and never would see.

"Alright, I'll see you later," she said.

He waved, shooed her away. Such turned, walked down the aisle. The girl with the braids and acne scars was gone from her post. There was no one to pay. She held the candles up to the security camera. "My friend's going to pay for these," she said to no one. The red light stared unblinking back at her.

The bell jingled when she opened the door, went back into the night. A weight leaned onto her back, pressed into her skin. Like being watched but this was the city, someone was always watching. The candles were unlit but hot in her hand for her crime of taking them. Such considered turning back but that weight, the eye weight, pushed her forward.

She was local, she'd pay in the morning if he didn't. Even if he did. Such walked to the corner. Put the candles into her backpack while she waited for the bus. She checked her phone, the bars were still low, bad signal. Did towers need electricity for the signal? It was summer, there were blackouts everywhere. She put the phone away.

The bus came, cool blue light pouring from the inside of it. She dug out a token, dropped it into the machine. The driver didn't look away from the road, closed the door behind her. They drove past the Stop N Shop. The strip of light over the stocked shelves flickered, went out with the streetlights and she couldn't see her neighborhood anymore.

There were always blackouts in the summer. The City didn't have enough power for everyone. But they made do. They drank lukewarm sodas and had parties.

She settled back into her seat, it was bound to come for them too.

The bus was empty, the glow too blue and cold without being cold. The air conditioner rattled, useless. Outside the world was black, impossible to see beyond the light. They might as well have been underwater, the glass was cool against her forehead. Such knew what was beyond the wide pane. The world was all run-down brick, faded paint, sad plastic and metal bus stops covered in Jesus Saves ads. Billboards rested on top of buildings. Banks, and luxury condos that didn't exist yet but would.

The bus passed from 55th to 54th. Midnight pitch black all around, the only light, the bus.

Black out.

By muscle memory she felt the stop coming. She pulled the yellow cord that ran the length of the bus, the bell chimed. The driver pulled to a stop and she stepped off through the back and onto the pavement. The bus pulled away, took its cold light with it and left her in the heavy, wet night.

Only a block from Leona's, Such knew the way, even without the comforting reminders of street signs. The City was connected in a thousand ways, nothing was ever far, just a bus and a block or two and some-times that felt like hours but everything was close in the City. Pressed up to and on top of each other. The

City was huge but it was a small thing to travel. A small thing to be inside.

And inside it was dark in the way the City was never supposed to be. Had never been. Midnight waves lapping at the curb, swallowing the bus and leaving her at the edge of an ocean. She couldn't see past it.

"Just my eyes," she said trying to blink the cold blue light out of them but the velvet void remained. She turned away. There was nothing to do but turn away.

She heard the laughter, the music as she came closer. Candles like the ones she carried were in half the windows. They stood open and she could hear laughter, singing, a baby crying in the needy warm way that they did. She stopped, breathed it in, the sound, the feel and behind her she heard nothing. It was only forward that the life was, that the world was. The City.

The door to Leona's building stood open and dark. Inside she could hear them, her friends and their friends. A glass encased candle. A novena, seven-day candle. St. Anthony, cloaked in green graced the front. Such reached into her little bag and pulled out the pack of white ones she'd brought. Lit one on the little flame and turned back to the street.

Empty, swallowed by the blackout, she couldn't see beyond her glow. The world was only what she held in her hand. Before her was an ocean, an undulating sea of nothing at all. Such sucked in her breath, entered the house.

Inside it was all laughter and music. Leona rented one room of many and the doors stayed open. It was darker than she thought but she could feel the other people, knocked into their sweat soaked bodies, inhaled them. The walls were covered with murals painted by artists long before Such had met Leona. There and gone before Leona had ever moved in. In the blank spaces there was art. Bits of costumes propped up in corners, hanging over chairs. Make up and impromptu altars of decadence scattered over tables and between them all were the bodies, hot and alive and dancing.

"Sorry! Sorry!" they laughed.

"Hey, have you seen TeeVee?" she asked grabbing hold of an arm, their drink splashing warm against her.

"Sorry, sorry!" they repeated and like the counter girl she didn't know if that was an answer or not. Sorry that they hadn't seen her, sorry that they'd knocked into her, or both. She couldn't make out their face. She couldn't make out any of their faces. They glowed and spun under fairy lights and dripping candles. Beautiful, awful angels in the velvet dark that seeped into the edges no matter how they spun the light.

She passed through the rooms, dodging wild arms, the light breaking from glitter adorned cheeks, silver and gold chains and hoops, wrapped and pierced through everything. Summer hot half naked bodies pulsed and pounded in time with the boom and bass that pumped through a synched line of battery powered speakers that would be dead by dawn.

But for now, it was all a party and there, across the living room, slipping up the stairs, twisting green braids disappearing into the second floor.

"TeeVee?" Such called into the hot sparkler filled darkness and the sound of a guitar being tuned answered her, mingled with laughter. No apologies here, she'd gone so far into it, the blackout licked at her heels, arms and legs bumped and caressed. She was anointed with alcohol and wax covered her hand like something holy.

TeeVee didn't answer but she thought she heard her. Took another flight to find her, the floor that Leona lived on. The little attic room where they'd smoked weed and fucked under the setting sun before they'd gotten their little apartment, their little life.

Like a princess tower, Leona's room was the furthest from the ground, the hottest space in the house. An exit to the roof through the window where they watched the sunrise. Not that first night but it didn't matter. Sunrise in the City was sunrise.

Sitting on her bed, smoking like always was Leona. "Hey, Such," she said. Tall and dark, hair in perfect curls that fell over her head, a mane. "Sorry. You missed her."

"Did she say where she was going?" Such asked dumbly.

"She didn't go anywhere. Nobody goes anywhere. Nobody leaves the city, not really."

"Then where is she?" Such asked. Her head swam, the air around Leona was heavy with sweet weed stench, like incense. Like a church.

Leona thumbed towards the window like she was hitching a ride. "Same place she always is, someplace she always was. Not you Such. Your art's real good. They like it out there," she pointed to glowing horizons. "You'll be ok."

Leona stood up stretched, stepping away her bed. Too dark to see her face. "Time for me to go back to the party. It'll be over in the morning and morning's coming soon." She left, closed the door.

Such looked at the window, wondered if the dawn was really false, wondered what time it was, how long she'd spent painting instead of enjoying. When she'd really missed TeeVee.

Outside the door she listened to the careening laughter, heard the music go askew. The blackout was spreading, taking the blocks of little run-down buildings, all those people barely hanging on. Swallowing them up to make room for the billboards, for the shop lights.

No room for art, for artist. Unless.

Unless the City saw you and they saw her. She could sit there till morning, when the sun lit up the world and the buses were running and make it back home to her empty apartment. She climbed out the window, found TeeVee, at last.

All around her the world was lightening, the true sun coming except for behind TeeVee where the world was a black square, like in Such's painting. Another door, another window. Where the world was night endlessly and the party never stopped. Or maybe it was nothing at all but TeeVee smiled and turned wordlessly, fearlessly.

A moment, Suchandsuch thought about the gallery show, where her painting had sold for more money than she'd ever seen, thought about how that meant she made it, that she'd get a chance to buy all the things that they'd wanted. To be all the things that they'd wanted.

All the things but together.

The hunger of the whole City, fed on them. In the morning the buildings would be empty, ready to be torn down, replaced with apartments that they couldn't afford.

In the morning all that would be left were paintings and make-up smeared clothing and the morning was there bright and beautiful and welcoming for her. The one who'd made it.

"Wait!" she called, rushed forward, reaching, grabbing for Teevee.

Suchandsuch's hand touched velvet blackout night. Wet, hungry City air that felt like the hot folds of TeeVee, the thick sweet press of her tongue and Suchandsuch never left the City.

Just This One Thing

Sara Century

IT WASN'T AN EYE IN THE BEGINNING, JUST A little bit of flesh, a bump on the wall. Marguerite ran her thumb over it again and again, then all her fingers. Everything in her bedroom was just the same as it had been yesterday, except this—this one thing.

She whispered a few disjointed words and looked around the dimly lit apartment. It still looked like the ad she'd seen online that prompted her to apply for the space three years ago, except that most of the light bulbs had gone out since and had never been changed. So it was all the same, just a little dimmer now, like most things.

She spent twenty minutes running her hands over the walls to confirm that there were no other patches of skin. It was the same as it had always been; a smooth, cold, bumpy, beige texture that could be concrete or plaster or anything. She thought, only briefly, about how odd it was to live in a place when you had no comprehension of how it held together. Maybe someone could pull a pin and topple the whole thing, and her room on the seventeenth (eighteenth?) floor would crash right into the street.

Marguerite sat at the edge of her bed and stared at the bump that was not yet an eye. "This is stressful," she muttered to herself and thought about starting a social media page just so she could write out the words "I'm very stressed about this" and know that someone would at least read it, even if they didn't understand or care.

As it was, she couldn't think of how to deal with it besides figuring out how to ignore it. She couldn't call anyone. She was curious to know if her landlord existed outside a seemingly endless series of odd notes that were left on her door at semi-regular intervals.

She winced to think of what would happen if they sent someone to take care of this. It would mean days or even weeks of people coming in and out of her apartment, and inevitably, she would be blamed for it. She ran through a series of possible excuses to explain this bizarre growth, bulletproof enough that no one could hold her liable for its existence. "It was just there one day," but no, that would not absolve her. "I think it has to do with the plumbing," but it was nowhere near any pipes. In the end, she lay down, and whispered, "This is not my fault."

The laptop in her office rang, and she suddenly remembered her call with Susan. She fell over herself rushing into the room, trying to achieve the veneer of normalcy. She pulled her hair back and smiled, then answered. "Hi, Susan!"

Susan had not made the same effort toward appearances. Her eyes were red-rimmed, as though she'd been crying not too long before, and her hands were noticeably shaking. "Hey, Margie," she said, but her voice was raspy. "How are things?"

Marguerite had "met" Susan online a couple of years before, not long after the first round of lockdowns began. Back when many had assumed that the extreme heat and constant influx of new viruses would eventually cease, plenty of people were desperate to find new ways to connect with others until things "returned to normal," whatever that meant.

Susan was an insurance broker who lived in London whose boyfriend had left immediately during the first lockdown when faced with the reality of being stuck in an apartment with her indefinitely. Since then, she and Marguerite had scheduled regular calls once or twice a month that would begin with general small talk and inevitably work into Susan asking Marguerite to role-play erotic banking scenarios with her, almost always based on the act of counting or touching money somehow. "Oh, yes, Miss Taylor, right away," Marguerite would say, flipping through a stack of paper she'd cut to make it look like dollar bills. They would each pull at their clothes and touch themselves until Susan reached over and ended the call, always without saying goodbye.

This had been going on for a long time now, and Marguerite knew it was a little odd but she hadn't felt a need to change anything. Susan was consistent, something easily written into a calendar, and she never left her to wonder what their interactions would consist of. For Marguerite, there was an emotional benefit to someone who only wanted one very specific thing from her, who wouldn't throw any curveballs her way.

"I'm good," Marguerite said, a shaky note in her voice after seeing Susan's distressed state. She'd hoped that answering the call would distract her from her own problems, but that seemed unlikely now, and she suddenly wished she'd never picked up. "Um, are you...how are you?"

"Not fucking great, Margie," Susan snapped, irritated enough that Marguerite didn't take the time to remind her that her name wasn't 'Marge' or 'Margie.' Susan continued, her voice softening, "Sorry, I'm just under a lot of stress at work. And my ex is-"

Marguerite's thoughts immediately returned to the

skin in the wall. It had been shocking to her when she first found it, but now her fingertips longed to feel it once more. She ran her hand over the top of her desk, some kind of plastic made to resemble wood, and tried to focus on Susan's incredibly mundane problems. She murmured, "Sorry to hear that," and "Oh, what an asshole," at what she hoped were the appropriate moments, but the distance between them seemed almost ludicrous to her at this moment. Not only was Susan across the ocean, not only would neither of them leave their apartments again any time soon, but she knew that Susan would just hang up if she tried to explain the bump on the wall.

There was an explosion in the background, close enough that Susan's camera shook. She looked genuinely alarmed and reached toward the screen. "Fuck! That one was close. The police tear-gassed the crowd so much last week that some of it got into the building. That had better not fucking happen again or I'll call... someone. I'd better go. Sorry... I'm just..."

Marguerite realized that she had started compulsively kneading the flesh right above her knee, and jumped when Susan knocked over a glass. "Um, no, it's-" she started.

Susan hung up.

Marguerite pulled the curtain back only a bit to see that the skies were still filled with smoke here as well.

The building had a sound filtration system to help keep the toxins from getting in. At least, that's what they said when she moved in. Things had gotten a lot worse since then, even if it'd only been a few years. She wondered if the air had changed without her noticing it, just a little at a time.

Just a little at a time, just this one thing.

By the next time she was scheduled to talk to Susan, the eye had opened, bloodshot, with a nebulous, ever-changing iris that wasn't a circle, instead branching out across the sclera like a web. Marguerite had made a game out of how long she could hold out in a staring contest, mumbling competitive threats at the eye. "I'm going to beat you this time," she swore, only to inevitably lose. The eye only closed when she wasn't looking.

Marguerite wondered what would happen if she attacked the eye in some way. She wondered if that wouldn't be a much more normal response than the one she found herself enacting, playing games with the eye, talking to it, hoping to befriend it somehow. Rather than being annoyed by its presence, the company enlivened her. She was more liable to dress up in the morning for work now even knowing she didn't have to. She talked aloud rather than keeping her thoughts to herself, thinking that it might benefit the eye to know what she was up to.

Life had been so lonely. Her parents, once so distant, and now dead. Her brother, a decade older and uninterested in forming a bond, her childhood friends off leading other lives now, her ex-boyfriend married with kids... an unfamiliar city rising around her and burning to the ground just a little more every day along with the rest of the world. From her window, she could see so much chaos and violence in the streets, but she believed sometimes that maybe even a hot gust of dirty air would feel good. Maybe the horror would be worth it, just to talk to another person again.

But now, she had the eye. She wondered if she wasn't underestimating the threat the eye could pose to her. It might have intended to harm her, but even when she searched her mind to its limits, she could not imagine anything worse than another three years alone in this apartment, performing a mundane data entry job for forty hours a week.

The act of organizing numbers clouded her brain, dominated her dreams, and defined her every waking moment. When off-the-clock, she worried about being back on, trying to mitigate her anxiety by clicking through order forms.

Once a week, she would walk to the end of the hallway to pick up her grocery delivery from an unseen worker. It would take time to work up the courage to walk out into the hall. She would rehearse a short script of what she would say if she bumped into one of her neighbors. In the time she'd lived there, she hadn't seen them much at all, only heard them crying or laughing now and again. They hadn't made a sound in a long time now, but she wanted to be prepared, just in case.

Her stomach would start to growl, and she would burst out the door and rush to get her packages. Back inside, she would ravenously eat from them, and only sometimes wondered what would happen if one day the packages didn't come at all.

The ringer went off, and she realized that her scheduled meeting with Susan had come around once again. She didn't immediately jump to answer as she was in the middle of a staring contest with the eye again. "You're lucky," she muttered finally. "I'll be back."

She fell into her office chair, tattered and falling into ruin. Not worrying about how she looked at all, she clicked into the call. She started to say "hello," but her voice caught in her throat as she attempted to decipher exactly what she was looking at.

Susan was dead – had been dead for a while, with a

blackish-green tint making it difficult to make out her features. There was blood spattered across the room, but it wasn't clear exactly where it came from. The call must have been automatic, Marguerite realized, then surprised herself by feeling slightly annoyed at Susan's insistence on allowing AI to control every little aspect of her life.

"Get it the fuck together, Susan," she whispered. Then she closed the window, thrilled to finally be hanging up on Susan and not the other way around. She went another step further and blocked the number. She stared at the blank screen for a bit, wondering if she should call someone to tell them about Susan before ultimately deciding against it. "What's one life, anyway," she wondered aloud, knowing that no one would call for her when she died, either. Instead, she went back to finish her staring contest with the eye.

MARGUERITE READ the notice she'd found taped to her door, again and again, trying to make sense of it. "Hello," then there was a blank space for them to personalize the letter where someone had written in the word 'tenant' rather than her name. "We're doing our annual apartment inspections and will be stopping by between August 11th at 5:00 am and August 28th at 5:00 am. Please be prepared for our visit! If you have any questions, call -" There was a space where they should have written a phone number that had been left blank, "Thank you for your cooperation. Signed, Royal Apartments Inc."

She immediately overwhelmed herself trying to think of a new script for this potential interaction. "What does one say to a building manager?" she wondered. "What is the appropriate greeting?" Should she say anything at all? Perhaps she could simply leave the door open and hide under a blanket until they left. What did they mean by "annual inspection" since no one had entered her apartment the entire time she had lived there?

Marguerite gasped suddenly, dropping the note. The most important thing would be to hide the eye. A series of horrific possibilities played out in her mind in which the landlord discovered the eye and tried to get rid of it by cutting it out or painting over it. This could not happen – she couldn't let it happen. She ran into her room. The eye was open and trained on her. She ran back to get the note, then showed it to the eye, not certain that it could read. It scanned the note as if it could, then looked back up to her. She shook her head.

The eye closed. Frustrated, she hit the wall with

her palm, then recoiled when she realized that she'd hit living flesh. The skin had spread, the patch now covering a couple of feet of space. She ran her hand over it, trying not to let the sensation distract her. She was stunned to discover four little nubs growing out of the wall underneath the eye, hidden by the nightstand.

Fingertips.

It took weeks for the building manager to show up. By then, the eyes had multiplied, with at least five at varying degrees of growth emerging from the wall. Part of a torso and an entire arm. She pulled out a tie-dye tapestry that she had bought in high school and placed it over the wall, apologizing to the eyes as they glared silently at her. "Don't give me that look," she whispered.

When he finally arrived, she realized that she couldn't have predicted the agitated mess of a person who showed up. Muttering to himself in the hallway and banging on the door like it was a matter of life and death rather than a routine apartment inspection, he looked like a cartoon drawing of a building manager, too on the nose to be real.

"Nate! Building manager! Open up!" he shouted.

She wondered why he hadn't stopped by any of the other apartments. She certainly would have heard him if he had. She went to open the door, but he used his key to barge in, flipping the light switch on and off. "You don't change the light bulbs?" he frowned, then waved the switch away in disgust. "I got to check some things. Have you had any issues?"

"Marguerite," she said, but then realized that he wasn't waiting for her name as he pushed past her, running his hand over a countertop and pulling back dusty fingertips.

"You don't use the kitchen much?"

"I haven't had any issues," she said. "I don't... I don't use the kitchen much, no."

"I can get you some light bulbs."

"I don't need them."

He paused, sneering slightly. "Right."

"I haven't met you before," she observed.

"Last guy died with the others in the suicide pact. I'm just checking on the still-living for the owner."

"The still-living?" Marguerite asked. "There are still... people here, right? I just...don't see anyone walking around or anything, so I... I wonder what they're... *how* they're doing."

"You're joking, right?" he said. "The building is just about empty. There's no one else on this floor anymore."

"I didn't hear anyone moving…"

He cackled, a hysterical tinge starting at the edges of his laugh and quickly working its way into the center. A moment passed where he seemed almost to be convulsing before he turned back to her. "They aren't moving anywhere anymore." He breathed hard for a few more seconds, then swallowed, calming himself. "I'm going to have to notify the owner about the crack in the door."

"It wasn't my fault," said Marguerite.

"Yeah," he replied, then continued with his inspection.

"How did… how did they…"

"Suicide pact," Nate said as if diagnosing a simple mechanical failure. "It's not the only one, it's happened in a lot of these kinds of buildings. Most of the ones they have me checking on are like this. They were all coordinated by the folks that lived here, except a few others and I guess you."

Marguerite felt a sharp sting of rejection for not having been invited to the mass suicide. Nate seemed uncomfortable and moved along.

"Anyway, it doesn't matter. I don't even know if the owner is still alive, to be honest, but the checks keep coming and I gotta do something, don't I?" He paused, then suddenly punched himself in the side of the head before he kept rifling through the kitchen as if nothing had happened.

She took a step back and sat down, watching him as he moved around the apartment. He knocked over a table but didn't seem to notice, and made marks on the notepad he'd brought with him. She heard him throwing things around in the bathroom and felt a pang of despair. At one time, both she and this man had been in a womb, connected to that parent's heartbeat, so much a part of someone else. And now... now, whatever this was.

She jumped to her feet when she heard him in her room, her sadness quickly shifting to horror. What would this man do if he found the eyes? She rushed to the doorway, stopping only to see him pulling aside the tapestry.

The first thing she realized was that new fingers were sprouting out underneath the arm, with maybe seven (eight?) new fingertips wriggling through the air. The second was that the arm had grabbed Nate by the neck and was choking him while the eyes gazed on. The new fingers reached toward him, too short to catch him but trying.

Marguerite considered doing something to stop them. The man hadn't hurt her, after all. He was unpleasant, but that wasn't worth dying for. Yet, even knowing this on an intellectual level, she couldn't overcome her sense of apathy. Instead, she watched as he died, whispering, "It's okay. Just go. It's okay." He tried to scream, kicking at her from where he hung, but it was pointless. When it was finally over, she stared into the eyes, and they stared back into her.

Even several minutes after Nate had stopped moving, the arm held fast. Marguerite focused on the hand. She leaned in, gently stroking the wrist, letting the ends of her hairbrush over the forearm. She breathed on the knuckles and saw a slight tremble rush over them. She pried the fingers off Nate's neck, gently, kissing the fingertips one by one as they reluctantly released his throat. She licked the palm, touching the wall with both hands. For a time, outside explosions rattled the windows and walls, but eventually, the apartment was quiet again.

Eventually, she would dispose of the man, cutting him into tightly wrapped pieces that could fit in the garbage. Detectives might have come asking about him at one time, but not now. Outside, sirens screamed, smoke filled the sky, and thousands of people flooded the streets. Watching from her window, she and the eyes may have been at the very center of the world.

Somehow, something was coming, through the metal exterior of the building, drifting into the air filters, up the seventeen (eighteen?) floors, past the locked door, through the cracks in the plaster. Growing eyes, hands, mouths, and tongues, hiding in the walls, bursting through and becoming something new. She couldn't stop it from coming. Steel girders and glass could contain her like a bird in a cage but it could never keep anything out; she understood that now. Every day, it came through just a little bit more. Every day, just a little closer than the day before.

The Spiraling Cadaver
Sam Richard

HE DIDN'T GET TO TALK WITH HER BEFORE SHE died because he missed her call. He doesn't remember her final message because he was drunk when he listened to–and then deleted–it. Like her final communication with him never happened.

Like she was never here.

And he wonders if maybe that's partially true. That maybe his memory isn't real, or at the very least isn't accurate. That the woman who he would give anything to see one more time had perhaps been more an amalgamation of several people experienced through the haze of alcohol and prescription pills.

Like he was never here.

But neither was the world. Or at least not really. That day the two of them watched another plane drop another bomb and another group of civilians seeking refuge were wiped clean off the map. No. Not clean. Horrifically so. Covered in dust and blood and cinder and ash. Found holding each other, trying to huddle in some kind of futile collective notion of safety. Bodies mangled.

Their bones shattered, protruding from gray flesh. No longer able to experience joy or love or hope or pain or sadness or self-righteousness or anger or greed or lust or friendship. People reduced to the things we were forged from. Clay and dirt and oil. Carbon. Water.

The human stain.

But the day the two of them watched another plane drop another bomb in another country, as they had year after year after year. As they all had. As we all have. Waiting for the planes and the bombs and the sorrow and the fear to finally come to them. To finally come on them.

They sat together, drinking a bottle of cheap corn whiskey she'd picked up on her way home. The delight in her eyes; the delight always in her eyes. But instead, they sat in silence once the bombs fell. Seemed like another day of horror, in that way that you might get used to over time.

Exposure therapy, but the dark inverse of that.
Numbness.
Inhumanity.

Shock.

Humanity.

Isolation.

Embrace.

They sat on their rickety, itchy couch exhausted from the day, from the week, from the month, and watched those fucking bombs fall. Eternal shall they reign.

They sat in silence. In pained awe. Not the awe of love and acceptance and abstract holy divinity, but awe of a truly biblical kind. Terrible and unknowable. The thing that melts your ability to think for hours or days or weeks or years or decades. Lifetimes. Generations. Centuries.

Just another day.

Always another fucking day. And another fucking bomb.

They watched it hit over and over from different angles like high quality porn. The money shot repeated in slow motion on television and on the internet for all the world to see. Look at how well we do this. *Look at how good we are. Look at how we fucking got them, enemies huddling together in their underground bunkers.*

It was too much; it was always too much, and she slammed another massive glug of the brown liquor and went to bed. Her head was pounding, tears threatening to break the surface tension of her eyelids. The images wouldn't go away. They were always there. If not that night, then the next night. And if not these people, then someone else. Someone who isn't them, but that doesn't make it ok. It just makes it empty and horrible and like the whole fucking world needs to stop and spin in reverse just to feel the mammoth weight of everyfuckingthing that it lets happen. That makes it happen. And we don't even pause; we don't hesitate.

The bed was soft and warm but hollow. All creature comforts rotting from the inside while the world remains–insists on being–this way. She cried herself to sleep, hoping for the numbness of exhaustion or booze or grief to take it away, to give her just a goddamn second to breathe without every gasping breath being full of abrasive, carcinogenic dust and irradiated powdered blood.

She could see the gray of their skin, the unmoving muscles underneath and nothing made sense. She fitfully slept with the images of the dead hovering over her, not as ghosts or apparitions, but as fully formed flesh and blood people who once lived and struggled and breathed the same rancid air as her; who once held the door open for a stranger and helped a child who'd tripped on a rock.

They sat with her as she slept.

But he watched the bombs fall. He couldn't rip

himself away. Not for her, not for anything. The way that feeling worms its way into your stomach and sends cold blood up to your heart. The way it hurts so fucking much but there's nothing else to do and every single channel and stream and article and video shows the same goddamn thing, but it grows increasingly clean and victimless. Our perfect, precise A.I. directed bombs only ever hit their intended targets who are always evil and against us and our allies and what we all stand for. And when they die, they are wiped from the earth like bleach to bacteria, not in a shower of rubble and shrapnel and rockets that shoot out literal knives that sever children's spines at weddings, but in a perfectly ordered way that leaves no trace left behind because there's a movie you should see and a new laptop that you need and are your erections hard enough and how's your testosterone level and didn't this celebrity do something so crazy recently?

That night, he let it move through his body like an orgasm. It hollowed him out, at least what was left to hollow out. Like the entire media-consumer interface was mainlined into him. Freebasing misery and consumer goods and pre-packaged opinions.

He popped another pill and downed it with a quarter of the bottle of whiskey.

The television his lullaby, his comfort, his everything.

The next morning she was gone. Nothing scary, just off to work. He could sense her warm lips on his cheek as he was waking up, as though she had just kissed him and was merely on the other side of the front door. Like she wasn't really gone, would never be gone but for this fleeting moment before they could be together again.

The television was still blaring. New images, new planes, new bombs, new victims. Not sure where. Same battle? Same country? Same American-made weapons - the only thing that leaves no doubts.

He went to the park to walk off some of the hangover, though a fifth of something in his pocket also helped. The cool air burned his lungs. He remembers that still. The way it stung. The way it constricted the tissue, making it harder to breathe like so much coal and burning rubber and melting plastic and toxic fumes.

A couple and their child walked by him, glaring at the bottle in his hand, but he was just glad to see other people around.

Isolation.

Fear.

Xenophobia.

Hate.

Suspicion.

All things perfected in the USA.

The park led to the bookstore and then to a restaurant and then to a bar and another and another and another. Drunk and alone, surrounded by strangers also wanting to connect but no longer knowing how, like the gears of socialization had been plenty lubed by the booze, but were too rusted in place for it to matter.

At least that's how it was for him.

Another handful of cheap beers and a few more pills, just to take the edge off, and the night went blank.

And then her calls, which he only knows from looking at his phone later. And then her message, which he only knows from looking at his phone later. And some ghost of her voice, but no clue what the words are or if they were even from that night. What if he's mixing together the cadence and rhythm of her voice from so many other conversations? An approximation of her essence.

What if that isn't what her voice sounded like at all. Now misshapen by time and grief and trauma and longing.

He only knows that the next day someone found her body in the woods. Her favorite woods. The deepest part of her favorite park on the far end of town. Dangling from a massive tree. Suicide. Her boots were off, on the ground beneath her feet.

She always loved to be barefoot.

No note.

Just the voicemail.

He panics when he thinks about it too much. When he imagines her alone in those woods, trying to decide if the world was too far gone and had given her nothing but pain and sorrow and misery despite what good there was. The thought of her calling and him not answering. Of that being the deciding factor. The terror rises in his chest, and he might pass out or puke or just start running and never stop. Which is what he did.

Only he did stop, at some point.

He popped more pills and downed them with the last of the liquor and ran until the hysteria in his heart was overrun by the pain pulsing through his body. Too much, too far, for too long, too hard, too painful, too exhausted.

He collapsed.

Woke up some time later. Dead phone. Unsure of where he was, how he got there.

Surrounded by echoing emptiness. And dirty, but somehow still shimmering tile.

Frozen escalators. Unmoving figures staring at him from behind grimy glass windows. He wanders the corridors, trying to figure out how he's gotten in. The memories so hazy and awful. Her bastard voice over and over in his ears speaking in the indecipherable tongues of a Pentecostal preacher.

The way her skin was so gray, just like the planes and the bombs and the buildings and the people crushed beneath them all. The weight of her hand in his, unmoving and unalive and unconvincing in the hope that she would just squeeze back, and everything would be ok again.

The mall stretches out in front of him eternally; storefront after storefront, to the point where they all bleed into one another. He tries to recall if he'd seen that same sporting goods store ten minutes ago, or if it was a different one, maybe by a different name. Different places, same font.

He tries to memorize each store he passes, taking special effort to say their names out loud to himself and the echo. *Hat Factory, Toys'A'Billion, Rejora, Antiqu, Freedom Clothing, Fjorsons.* Each store different, but he always forgets in about twelve entries what the others had been.

Endless shopping experiences. All gated off and dark inside. All covered in dust and grime. Ash and cinder.

Maybe blood, too.

An abandoned cathedral to our highest religion. He passes an electronics store with one lone high-def flat-screen tv on. More planes, more bombs, more fanfare and reverie. More technology that he holds dead in his pocket helping lead the way. More gray and broken, nameless, faceless bodies. We rarely see the reality of their grief, much less in their joy, in their celebrations, in their daily lives. *We got'em!* on the screen. More shit and misery and death and pain and emptiness. More human inhumanity evolving into inhuman inhumanity by way of drones and artificial intelligence. Same blindness, but now with shiny new toys.

The television manufactured by the same company that made the bombs and the planes and the cameras recording it. The same company that owns the store in the mall and the real estate investment firm that owns the mall and has controlling shares in the studios who are advertising their films on the same television networks showing the bombs who also own the delicious and refreshing soda advertised after the movie trailer. The films produced in conjunction with the Pentagon who have final cut rights just so there's nothing subversive in there, but it's worth it because the film company gets to use their planes and tanks and aircraft carriers. The same planes that are dropping the bombs. And the heroes smile with perfectly white teeth and nary a spot of blood for the victorious and brave efforts fighting more bad guys halfway across the world.

Her voice distorts more in his ears. Her laugh is gone from his memory.

He keeps going. More filthy glass. More tangles of

escalators. So thirsty, he lets the final drop of metallic whiskey tingle his tongue, parching his throat further.

Down a few more corridors, to nowhere in particular. To nothing in particular, just hoping for fresh air and the sky overhead. Hitting a center, of sorts, in the mall sits a fountain. The water is thick and congealed with time. Filling up his bottle, he takes a swig. Warm and unappealing, but salty in a refreshing way that makes no sense in his mouth and down his throat.

He pops another few pills and treks forward, into the unknown of the mall. More storefronts bleeding together into others. *Have I been this way before?* His phone vibrates in his pocket. His dead phone.

A voice message. He hits play.

It's her voice again, ringing in his ears. Not a known language. Tongues, gibberish. It's coming from the phone, but filling the empty, endless halls. Her voice meets the echo and they dance across the marble floors, glass, and tile walls. They shimmer in the majesty of acoustics, bounding and bouncing from one corridor to the next.

Like a knife to the soul.

He tries to turn it off, but his phone stares blankly at him. Breathing, speaking, dead. It pulses in his hand like something's crawling through it.

Her echo walks with him. He drinks more of the thick salty water and gags down a couple more pills until the bottle is empty. He tosses it with a skid that joins in the chorus around him.

He walks and walks and walks. *Forest-Mart, Pretzel Man, Cliniq, Vertigo, Roberth's Shoes.* A never-ending array of options that don't repeat, of this he's now sure.

Shifting waves of gray sand blow in across the marble, the wind sharing in the glee of the echo and her voice and the skittering. His movements grow slow and tedious in the heavy grit. Great heat rises from nothing and nowhere. Loud popping in the distance. The shop windows are scuffed and scratched by the abrasive dust, which slowly climbs up the side of the glass, getting higher and higher until it's up to his thighs.

His mind occupied with the everything and the nothing of it all, so much so that he almost misses the open door to one of the shops. *Red Owl.* Mannequins in hiking gear stare out at him from the doorway and through the glass. Entering, he closes the door behind him, trying to stop the slow pour of sand from gaining any more ground in the relatively unscathed outdoors store.

The echo isn't as loud in there, but her voice still drones, reduced back to what it was before the mall. The incessant cry to be heard, the mystery within his own fragile mind. The specter that will never leave.

The droning of a television from the other side of the room. Slowly, he follows, trying to keep his focus on signs of life for the first time since he arrived.

How long has it been? Could they be opening soon? Maybe a chance to find someone who knows where an exit is. But are they open at all? Is there a 'they' who are coming?

But then fear, coiling up underneath the questions, pushing down his throat like so many filthy, jagged fingers.

More planes and more bombs and more buildings and more people turned to nice, clean dust before a snapshot of how this soda will save the world if someone were to only listen and that massive gasoline companies are doing their best to keep the environment safe and clean and how exciting it is that your favorite corporate banking institutions now has queer friendly commercials and don't you love it and maybe you should join the Marines, you are a real man after all, aren't you?

Something moves behind the tv. Frozen, unsure what to do, he wants to call out, but he can't hear himself over her voice and the incessant bombs and gray-skinned children being carried by their broken wailing mothers and this delicious new taco is available up until 3:00 AM at the drive-through and why didn't he just answer the fucking phone and why didn't he just answer the fucking phone and why didn't he just answer the fucking phone and up next on the news are your children in danger–here's how–and why doesn't he remember her last message and why can't he understand her words and why the fuck did she die oh god why did she fucking kill herself what the fuck did I do why is this happening and you should invest in gold and I just want her to be here again even if it means we can't be together I just need to know that she can be out existing in the world living her life in hope and dreams and love and pain and hardship and all the things that come with being alive but what the fuck this shouldn't be part of it and can she just come back and I'll take her place I don't even fucking care I just want it all to end.

And maybe it does.

And maybe it doesn't.

Because he'll never know because I'll never know and we keep doing this over and over and nothing fucking changes. More death. More shiny new weapons. More new sneakers to buy. More endless fucking malls invading our waking lives. None of it meaningful. None of it necessary.

Just like her death.

And several figures appear, covered in camping clothing with the tags still on. They're gaunt and gray, like their flesh has mummified under packed layers of dry sand. Eyeballs receded to the point of invisibility; lips pulled back in jagged, leathery layers exposing dry rotting teeth. Dust billows off of them as they move. They don't speak. They just observe. Their attention split between him and the images on the television and their phones. The high-def flat-screen that pulses with comfort and warmth, that invites him in to join them just as they invite him in to join them. Not with words. Unspoken warmth. Unspoken comfort. The videos on their phones flash in unison with each other. With the television. One broken image at a time.

And he's not alone. They bask in the unnatural glow and watch the shiny planes and their funny bombs and the cartoon villains who get hurt but come back week after week with more new hijinks and plots. And there is no dust or blood or shattered lives or dead children anymore. There are no more grieving families wondering how to even begin to have a future in all this hatred and chaos and death. There is only warmth and comfort and light.

About the Authors

Scott Dwyer is a writer, critic, and publisher from Upstate New York. He runs Plutonian Press, a small press specializing in weird horror and dark erotica. He also runs a website, The Plutonian, where you can find essays and articles on horror in literature and film, movie and book reviews, and interviews. You can find The Plutonian and Plutonian Press books at theplutonian.com

Joe Koch writes literary horror and surrealist trash. Their books include *The Wingspan of Severed Hands*, *Convulsive, The Shipwreck of the Cerberus*, and *The Couvade*, which received a Shirley Jackson Award nomination in 2019. His short fiction appears in numerous publications including *Vastarien, Southwest Review, Children of the New Flesh*, and *The Book of Queer Saints*. In addition, they co-edited the art horror anthology *Stories of the Eye* with Weirdpunk Books. Find Joe (he/they) online at horrorsong.blog and on social media sites as horrorsong

Brendan Vidito is the author of the Wonderland Award-winning collection, *Nightmares in Ecstasy* (Clash Books, 2018) and *Pornography for the End of the World* (Weirdpunk Books, 2022). He also co-edited the Splatterpunk Award-nominated anthology *The New Flesh: A Literary Tribute to David Cronenberg* (Weirdpunk Books, 2019) with Sam Richard. He lives in Ontario. You can visit him at brendanvidito.com

Donyae Coles is a horror and weird fiction writer. Her debut novel, *Midnight Rooms,* is releasing in Summer of 2024. You can follow her on Twitter @okokno or on her website, donyaecoles.com

Sara Century is a writer and filmmaker who has co-founded the Bitches On Comics podcast, the Decoded Horror Podcast, and the production company Sympathetic Lightning. Her first short story collection *A Small Light & Other Stories* is available through Weirdpunk. Find out more at saracentury.com

Sam Richard runs Weirdpunk Books and is the author of *Grief Rituals, Sabbath of the Fox-Devils,* and the Wonderland Award-Winning Collection *To Wallow in Ash & Other Sorrows.* He is the editor of several anthologies, including the Splatterpunk Award-Nominated *The New Flesh: A Literary Tribute to*

David Cronenberg, *Stories of the Eye*, and *Cinema Viscera*. His short fiction litters the landscape of various anthologies and magazines. Widowed in 2017, he slowly rots in Minneapolis. You can stalk him @SammyTotep on socials or www.weirdpunk-books.com

Also from Weirdpunk Books

Elogona - Samantha Kolesnik

An evocative tale of sapphic love in a post-apocalyptic world dominated by religious zealots and supernatural monsters.

Kolesnik's *Elogona* transports readers to a time after the world's end, when a long-dormant sea creature has awoken to stake its claim against one of the last human settlements.

Verna must battle both man and monster to protect her family and her newfound love for Audrey, a refugee from the mainland.

Meanwhile, the Elogona calls...

Chaindevils - Matthew Mitchell

Embrace the chaos with Matthew Mitchell's debut novella, which tears off pieces of horror, grimdark fantasy, dying earth fiction, and drug literature, and smashes them together in hazy, mud-coated ways unlike anything you've ever seen.

"Mitchell pens a wild extrapolation of a post-apocalyptic North American Landscape by way of *The Road*, *Warhammer 40k*, and pulp westerns. *Chaindevils* is hard, grisly fare."

Laird Barron (*The Wind Began to Howl*)

Mutant Circuit - Mark Jaskowski

What is happening to Katherine?

Someone put something into her at the plasma center and took it back out again. By the time her friends catch up to her, she's not exactly the person they remember. She has begun to change into something new, and if they're going to help her escape the people who did this to her, they may need to transform, too.

Squarely in both the crime and body horror traditions, *Mutant Circuit* reads like Elmore Leonard and David Cronenberg meeting at 3 AM in a run-down strip-mall parking lot, and Mark Jaskowski is the conspirator who brought them there.

*Thank you for picking up this Weirdpunk book!
We're a small press out of Minneapolis, MN and our
goal is to publish interesting and unique titles in all
varieties of weird horror and splatterpunk, often from
queer writers. It is our hope that if you like one of our
releases, you will like the others.
If you enjoyed this book, please check out what else we
have to offer, drop a review, and tell your friends
about us.
Buying directly from us is the best way to support what
we do.
www.weirdpunkbooks.com*